NEW YORK TIMES BESTSELLING AUTHOR TRACEY JANE JACKSON WRITING AS

PIPER DAVENPORT

REESE

A DOGS OF FIRE STORY

Sale of this book without a front cover may be unauthorized. If this book is coverless, it may have been reported to the publisher as "unsold or destroyed" and neither the author nor the publisher may have received payment for it.

Reese is a work of fiction. Names, characters, places, and incidents are the products of the author's imagination and are used fictitiously. Any resemblance to actual events, locales, or persons, living or dead, is entirely coincidental.

Cover Art
Jack Davenport

ISBN-13: 9781670126832

Published in the United States

REESE

A DOGS OF FIRE STORY

It took a LOT of thought before I decided to take the plunge and change the cover to this book…because I LOVED the original cover, but unfortunately, it looked more "chick lit" than romance, so it made more sense to put a cover on this book that better suited the story. Since I can't fully let it go, though, here's the original…just so it's never forgotten.

All it took was one page and I was immediately hooked on Piper Davenport's writing. Her books contain 100% Alpha and the perfect amount of angst to keep me reading until the wee hours of the morning. I absolutely love each and every one of her fabulous stories. ~ Anna Brooks – Contemporary Romance Author

Get ready to fall head over heels! I fell in love with every single page and spent the last few wishing the book would never end! ~ Harper Sloan, NY Times & USA Today Bestselling Author

Piper Davenport just reached deep into my heart and gave me every warm and fuzzy possible. ~ Geri Glenn, Author of the Kings of Korruption MC Series

JBJ – Love doing life with you, baby.

Alexa

Portland, Oregon
Eight years ago…

FOR AS LONG as I can remember, my mother has always told me that I was a descendent of the House of Romanov, but unless there was a survivor from the massacre, it would be impossible. But Mama loved her stories and you didn't argue with Mama or you'd find yourself on her "list," so we always played along.

I might not have been imperial by blood, but I *was* Mob royalty…a fact I abhorred. And because of my "royal" connections, I had several secrets I was forced to keep. The biggest one being that I'd fallen in love with the son of a notorious biker and if my father discovered our secret, he'd kill him…then me. I was seventeen, after all, and couldn't possibly know my own mind. My father had all the power when it came to my life…the father who killed people who defied him, so I was kind of stuck.

My parents moved to the US from Russia one year before my brother was born, and they'd quickly acclimated to their new life, taking over most of the West Coast while managing to keep me in a protective bubble. The bubble had burst the second I'd met Reese Alden and he explained a few things to me about how the world of one-percenter motorcycle clubs and Mobs worked.

"*Lex*!" my brother snapped.

Sergei pulled me from my thoughts and I narrowed my eyes at him. "Yes, darling brother?"

"Her name is Alexa, Sergei," Mother said. "Don't make me remind you of that again."

"*Da*, Mama," he said, and met my eyes again. "*Alexa*. Are you going to homecoming with Vlad?"

It was family dinner hour (or, as Sergei and I referred to it, the witching hour), so it was imperative we played the adoring children, even if it was far from the truth.

"No," I said (for the umpteenth time). "I'm not going anywhere with Vladimir Kozlov, Sergei, we've had this conversation before."

"I'd like you to go with him," Father said, his Russian accent heavier than usual, an indication he was tired.

I scowled at Sergei. This was his doing, the little bastard. I schooled my features and faced my father with a serene smile. "Papa, Vladimir is not respectful to me, and I'd rather not subject myself to his wandering hands."

My father set his knife and fork down and wiped his mouth with his napkin. "He touches you?"

"Alexa," my brother hissed under his breath.

I ignored him.

"Yes, Papa. Often. It's disgusting," I whispered. "And he scares me."

My brother let out a painful groan, albeit quietly, but I refused to let it affect me. I *had* to get the Kozlovs off my father's radar in reference to an appropriate family match. If I didn't, the second I turned eighteen, I'd be forced to marry Vlad.

"He scares you," Father said, his voice pitched low.

"Da, Papa."

"I will take care of this."

Okay, maybe I'd gone too far. I wanted Vlad off my back, not dead.

"Papa, please don't hurt him," I rushed to say. "I'm sure he doesn't mean to scare me."

"*Solnyshko*, I will take care of it."

Well, crap. Whenever Papa called me his small sun, he was on optimum protect Alexa mode.

"*Spasibo*, Papa."

"Pretty sneaky, sis," my brother whispered for my ears only.

I glanced at him out of the corner of my eye and he was mentally stabbing me to death…I knew he was. I knew this look all too well, over far too many games of Battleship and Connect Four. Pretty sneaky sis, indeed.

Vladimir was a friend of his…a disgusting,

douchebag friend, but still a friend. I sighed internally. I'd need to figure out how to minimize the damage somehow.

Dinner finally wrapped up (thank God) and we were excused. My brother grabbed my arm and dragged me up to our suite of rooms, pulling me into his room.

"Does Vlad really touch you?"

"*Yes*," I said. "All the time. How do you not know this?"

"Maybe because you didn't tell me."

I sighed. He was right. "I'm really sorry, Sergei. I should have."

"Damn it!" He dragged his hands through his hair. "Dad's the least of his problems."

"I don't want him dead," I insisted. "I just want him to stop harassing me, so if you can figure out a way to make that happen, I'll love you forever."

He gave me a wry grin. "You'll love me forever even if I don't."

"This is true. You're kind of a big deal in my life."

"I'll take care of it."

"Thank you."

"Am I still driving you to Paisley's?"

I nodded. "That would be great."

My parents refused to let me get my license. They felt it was the man's job to drive, so I was at the mercy of my brother or one of Papa's drivers, to take me wherever I needed to go. It sucked.

"Grab your stuff," Sergei said. "Let's get out of here before they stop us."

I was already packed for my overnight with Paisley. No one knew I wasn't actually planning on being there the entire night, but that's what best friends were for…cover. Especially when said friends had parents who were rarely home.

Paisley Bell had been my best friend since I was ten. We'd met while attending the same private Catholic school and we'd been close despite the fact she was "normal." I'd been raised to never speak about my father's business…not that I was told much, but I was an inquisitive child and found out things I shouldn't have. The only two people I ever told anything to were Paisley and Sergei.

I kissed my parents and then followed Sergei to the car. We drove in comfortable silence to Paisley's home in the West Hills of Portland and Sergei walked me to the door. Paisley's parents were out for a few hours, but my mother had spoken to her mother, so the overnight was sanctioned since Paisley's parents would be home before midnight.

Paisley pulled open the door and grinned. "Hi, guys."

My best friend was gorgeous with a capital G, and I smiled as Sergei suddenly got taller. He adored her, but she had no time for him, which was good for him. My brother needed to be taken down a peg or two on the conceit board.

"I'll see you tomorrow," I said, then slipped into the house and closed the door.

"You're cutting this close, Lex," Paisley warned.

"I know." I bit my lip. "Dinner took a little longer than expected."

Paisley peeked out the living room window. "Your brother's gone."

"Okay." I glanced at my watch. "Five minutes."

Four minutes and fifty-eight seconds later, I heard the sweet sound of Harley pipes, and hugged Paisley before rushing out the front door and around the corner. My breath hitched as I watched Reese swing his leg off his bike and remove his helmet.

Good gravy, I loved him with everything I had. I made a run for him, his arms coming around me as I slammed against him, kissing him deeply. "Ohmigod, I've missed you, sugar bear."

Reese was nineteen and had always reminded me of a Norse god. Shaggy, dark hair, soft to the touch, fell over his forehead shielding his deep blue eyes when he desired it to. Never to me, though. I always got his full attention when he was with me. I'd given him his nickname mostly because it had irritated him and he got the cutest look on his face whenever I used it…but now he was so used to it, his look was gone, replaced with an expression of loving resignation.

He chuckled. "Missed you too, Freckles."

I was a sucker for his nickname for me, partly because he was such a badass and there was nothing sexier than a biker badass calling me "Freckles." But mostly because it was said in such reverence. I used to hate my freckly face until he informed me it was one of his favorite things about me.

His father and my father were the same. Oh, Papa would say that John "Brick" Alden was far below him, but my father killed people for a living while trafficking drugs, and so did Reese's. The only difference was, my father flaunted his wealth, giving the impression he was high-class, while Reese's dad was part of the Gresham Spiders, a nasty and gruff motorcycle club, indicating he didn't care what impression he gave.

I'd met Reese when my brother dragged me and Paisley to a bonfire out at Cannon Beach two years ago. Reese and his buddy, Ryder, were already on the beach and they had beer. My brother and his friends sniffed them out in zero point two, and Paisley and I had no choice but to go along for the ride.

I'd ended up talking to Reese all night. I was surprised to discover he didn't really drink much…he said his dad was an angry drunk and he didn't want to turn out like him.

After that, our relationship was an exercise in subterfuge, which admittedly, made things a little more exciting.

"How long we got?" Reese asked after he stopped kissing me.

"Until midnight."

"Okay, Cinderella, let's roll."

After another kiss, he handed me a helmet and a leather jacket, then I climbed on his bike behind him. Reese drove me to our private make-out hill overlooking Portland. Despite the cold, I felt warm, especially when Reese pulled an oversized sleeping bag out of his saddlebags.

"Is this thing going to give you enough room to get a good smack or two in?" I asked.

"Fuck, baby. Seriously?" he asked, and I couldn't help but notice his growing erection.

I giggled. I had just discovered I loved having his hand connect with my ass…like, I thought about it constantly, and demanded it anytime we had sex. It had all happened about six months ago when we'd been at Paisley's parents' beach house. Paisley and her boyfriend at the time invited us up for the weekend, and they left us alone in the house for a couple of hours. Reese had playfully smacked me as we headed into the bedroom and I attacked him, ripping off my clothes and begging him to do it again. Because the thought of hurting me (even when I begged for it) was abhorrent to him, it took some convincing, but now we both looked forward to our version of a little kink.

"Yes, seriously," I said.

Reese shook his head. "That stays behind closed doors, I think."

I wrinkled my nose, but didn't argue. He was probably right. I'd be mortified if we were caught naked in public.

Reese flicked open the sleeping bag, wrapping us in the warmth, and then we sat down and stretched out on the grass. Reese pulled me over his chest and kissed me gently. "We're gettin' out."

"Getting out of what?"

"The Club. Ryder and me."

I sat up with a gasp and stared down at him. "How?"

He closed his eyes for a second and then opened them again. "Very carefully."

This wasn't good. I'd met Ryder only once at the beach the night Reese and I met, along with a few of his buddies, and Reese had said that was on purpose. He was also trying to keep our relationship quiet in an effort to protect me.

"Reese," I whispered. "That's great…but it scares me."

"I know…it's why we gotta quit this for a bit."

"We've gotta quit what?" I asked, although, I knew what he was saying.

"Shit," he rasped.

"Shit, what?" I demanded.

"Lex—"

"Are you breaking up with me?" I snapped, and

tried to get distance from him.

Reese held firm. “Not forever. I just need to get clear. I don’t wanna drag you into any of this. If Brick gets you on his radar, you’re in danger.”

“No one can touch me.”

He sat up and stroked my cheek. “Baby, that’s not true.”

“I don’t want to stop ‘this.’ I love you. We can figure this out together.”

“I can’t take that risk.”

“Ohmigod, Reese, nothing’s going to happen to me. My dad’ll make sure of it.”

He dragged his hands down his face. “You don’t know Brick.”

“And you don’t know my dad.” I pulled his hands from his face. “*Hello*, Russian Mob.”

“I’m not willing to take a chance with your life, Lex.”

“It’s not your call to make.”

“Yeah, baby, it is.”

“You’re willing to throw this away because you’re afraid?” I challenged.

He swore and shook his head. “Goading me isn’t the way to go here, Lex.”

I threw my hands up in the air. “Gah! You’re so bossy.”

“I have to get out without having to worry about you.”

“You don’t have to worry about me,” I argued.

“All I ever *do* is worry about you!” he snapped. “Goddammit, Lex. I’m consumed with making sure you don’t ever get on Brick’s radar.” He stroked my face. “If he knew about you, he’d either kidnap and ransom you to your father, or he’d kill you for fear of what I may have told you about the Spiders. When my father gets his way, someone else always gets hurt, and I can't let that someone be you."

I'd conceded that, because our world was different than most, and Reese knew his dad, but it didn't mean I agreed with his decision. "Okay, I get it. But I don't understand why you're going overboard on this. We've kept our secret for two years. We can keep it for longer."

He shook his head. "If I start the process of getting out, Brick's going to be even more of an asshole, gettin' in my business more than he already is. I won't take that chance."

"But it could take years."

He sighed. "I'm aware."

"You're willing to be separated from me for *years*?" I challenged.

"If it means you're alive, hell yeah."

I blinked back tears. "Then we're done."

"Lex—"

"No. You either love me enough to figure it out *with* me or you walk away." My bravado was impressive, considering I didn't mean any of it.

Reese studied me for several tense seconds before he gave me a curt nod and rose to his feet.

"Seriously?" I hissed.

"I'll take you back to Paisley's."

"Wait. I didn't mean it."

He grabbed the sleeping bag and rolled it up.

"Don't do this," I whispered, standing slowly.

"Don't have a choice, Lex."

"Yes you do. You always have a choice."

He shook his head and I felt panic and devastation fill my heart. How did I ever believe he was the real deal? God, I was *such* an idiot. He'd probably planned to hit it and quit it all along. Granted, he'd been hittin' it for a year, and was just now quitting, but still, I should have known he'd dump me.

"Come on, Lex."

"Fine."

I straightened my shoulders, donning my safety gear, and climbing on the bike without comment. As Reese drove me back to Paisley's, I couldn't fully process what had just happened. We couldn't really be over, could we? He was the love of my life, but now I felt like our whole relationship had been a sham…he'd lied to me from the get-go and I wanted to die. When Reese pulled the bike to a stop, I threw my helmet at him, walked into my best friend's surprised arms, and sobbed for the next three hours.

* * *

Reese

After dropping Lex off at Paisley's, I forced myself not to run after her. Fuck, I loved that woman more than life, but if she got hurt (or worse) because I didn't let her go, I'd never be able to live with myself. I just needed a little time to make things safe for us. Ryder and I had a plan. It was a good plan.

Little did I know the plan would take a hell of a lot longer than any of us expected.

Alexa

Present day...

I GOT PINCHED...popped...nabbed by the five-0... jammed up by the po-po. Since I'd never been in trouble with the law before, I wasn't sure which phrase best fit my current situation. All I knew was I was now sitting in holding at the Multnomah County Detention Center, handcuffed to a pretty biker babe who looked like she was having an even rougher night than me. I couldn't blame her for her constant stares; she must have been weirded out being chained to a nun. Why wouldn't she? Even though I was currently chained up in a den of sinners, I was dressed like a saint.

"What are you in here for?" she asked as I gnawed

off the fingernails of my free hand. One had started to bleed, but I welcomed the pain.

I studied the damage, before smiling at her, "Drugs."

The woman's eyes widened.

"Oh, well, family, really. Family leading me to drugs I suppose," I replied, somewhat lost in thought. I was still trying to make sense of the whole situation myself.

She snorted. "I feel you. Being around my family would drive me to drugs too."

"Oh, no, sorry. Not *my* drug problem...well, since I'm in here, I suppose it kind of became my drug problem. My stupid-ass brother." I covered my mouth. Nuns really shouldn't swear. "Sorry. I'm working on my swearing problem."

"No judgment here," she said.

I smiled. "Thanks. I'm Al—I mean, Sister Maria."

"I'm Ashley," she replied sweetly. Unlike most of our fellow "guests," the two of us appeared to be the only sober ones in the police station. She sounded like a nervous wreck and I could hardly imagine what she could have been in here for.

"What'd you do?" I asked in a way that made me feel like a character in a bad mobster movie.

"Trusted the wrong asshole."

I sighed, Reese's face swimming before me. "Been there, done that."

Ashley's eyes widened, but before she could comment, an officer took her away to be booked. I went back to annihilating my nail beds and shook my head.

How the hell did I end up here? *Oh, yeah, I remember. Stupid Sergei.*

So much had happened in such a short amount of

time, I was still not entirely sure if I was living in reality or if my life was really some made for Lifetime movie. I'd started a really great law career two years ago. It was the fulfillment of a dream finally coming to fruition, despite my shattered heart. However, shortly after I'd found my place and groove with my new job, the life I'd carefully rebuilt crumbled again.

Almost a year ago, my father had been murdered by the next in line for the mob crown and Sergei, our mother, and I had gone into hiding. Right after my father was killed, there had been a rumor going around that my mother was next on the list. Whether or not that was true, I didn't know, but the thought was scary and it was why we were all separated…and safe. That was until Sergei bartered for our lives.

Idiot.

And I say that with all love and devotion, but seriously, he sold his soul to the Russian mob for me and I wish he hadn't.

Which brought me to here…indirectly.

* * *

Gone was my sheltered world of armed bodyguards and more money than God (Father's words, not mine), replaced by some skuzzy rat-infested flophouse.

I didn't know what time it was, all I knew was it had been at least two days since I'd been taken from the FBI safe house I was being housed in, and beaten into unconsciousness by one of my father's cronies. I was hungry, thirsty, and I had to pee.

"Lex," Paisley whispered beside me.

Paisley actually shouldn't be here and, quite frankly, I was pissed she was. After I'd agreed to be a material witness against the Mob's nefarious businesses, the FBI had whisked me and my family away without a word to anyone we knew. Paisley, however, was also inquisitive...only, she had P.I.-type skills and found me. Seriously, this chick should be a spy. But the problem with this side of her personality was it got her snatched as well.

"Are you okay?" I asked.

"I'm pretty sure my arm is broken," she rasped. "I can't really feel anything now."

Paisley groaned, but we were both chained to a metal ring bolted to the floor and couldn't move more than a few feet away from the wall. After I woke up the first time, I'd tried to figure out a way to get out, but didn't have a way to unscrew the bolts, so we were stuck.

I knew we had captors because I'd heard several men's voices while I was in and out of consciousness. We also had water and crackers delivered a few times a day as well.

I was aware there were others being held here. I'd heard crying and voices, and some of the voices sounded young. I was disgusted. One of the reasons Papa had been killed was he refused to have any part in trafficking and prostitution. Trafficking drugs he was fine with, people, not so much.

"Lex, I'm really scared," Paisley whispered.

"I know, honey. I am too."

"How are you so calm?" she accused.

"I'm not," I said. "I'm just trying to think one or two steps ahead of whoever took us, but I can't do that if I allow myself to freak out."

"Do you mind if I do?"

"Have at it, honey, just do it really quietly."

Before Paisley could respond, gunfire sounded, then yelling and screaming (not from us, which shocked the hell out of me), so I pulled her down and covered her with my body.

"What the hell?" Paisley let out a frustrated grunt and pushed me off. "Why would you do that?" she snapped.

"Sorry. Instinct."

"Well, don't be an idiot, Lex."

The door of our prison slammed open and a large man filled the doorway. "Two in here!" he yelled into the hallway.

Paisley and I jumped in fright, huddling closer together. The thought of being taken to yet another location did not sit well with me, especially with Paisley needing medical attention.

"What do you want?" I demanded, my false bravado on hyperdrive.

The man approached us, and I couldn't help myself from sliding slightly in front of Paisley. This earned me a painful flick to the ear. I ignored it.

"I'm here to help," he said. "I'm Agent Cameron Shane. We're getting you out of here."

"We?" Paisley asked.

He hunkered down in front of us and pulled out a handcuff key. "The FBI."

I gasped and shook my head. "No. Leave us alone!"

Cameron frowned. "Ma'am, you're safe. No one's going to hurt you."

"I don't think he's one of them, Lex," Paisley said.

"I'm not taking any chances," I hissed.

Cameron held his hand out and Paisley settled hers in it. He unlocked her handcuff and she grabbed for her broken arm, cradling it to her chest.

He turned to me and I tentatively reached my arm out. He uncuffed me and I wrapped my arm around my best friend.

* * *

The slam of a cell door brought me back to the present.

After we had been rescued, Paisley got to go home, but I was now being hidden in a Catholic abbey in Oregon, along with several other young women who'd been held in the flop house. I also had a "handler." Agent Cameron Shane. Tall, dark, and drop-dead gorgeous, the FBI agent was all alpha all the time, über professional, and just the right amounts of Boy Scout and altar boy. He also lived in Portland and I adored him. I'd had to give up my law career…at least for the moment, and I had no idea when I'd be able to get back to it.

I dropped my head back against the wall and squeezed my eyes shut. My mother had limited contact with me (we were still separated and could only communicate on approved days and using burner phones). She'd called me on a non-approved day, frantic because she couldn't reach my brother, and like an idiot, I sneaked out of the convent and to one of his favorite places to "disappear," and right into a drug deal. A drug deal that was broken up by the local police.

Sergei and I had been taken away in separate police cars and I was pretty sure I'd never see my brother again.

A police woman approached me and gave me a smile. "You're free to go," she said, and unlocked my handcuffs.

"Really? I thought I had to get booked."

"You have a friend in the FBI, apparently. So, you get to miss the entertainment of central booking," she said. "Someone's waiting to take you back to the convent. He's out front."

I followed the police officer out to the front, expecting to see Cameron, and my breath left my body.

"No," I ground out. "Absolutely not."

Reese Alden, the man who shattered me almost eight years ago, stood glaring at me. I almost turned around to demand the officer take me back to a cell.

I turned to head to the desk to find someone else to help me.

"Nice try," Reese growled, and grabbed my arm.

My head swam with questions. What was Reese doing here? Where had he been for the past eight years? How did he know I was in jail? How did he know I was at the convent…no one was supposed to know that.

Did he miss me? Ohmigod, I shouldn't care if he missed me. He'd ripped my heart out of my chest and stomped on it with his unbelievably sexy motorcycle boots.

"You're coming with me," he said.

"Um, no, no I'm not." I tried to rip my arm from his hold, but to no avail. He kept me immobile without hurting me as he gently dragged me toward a side door. "Reese," I hissed. "Stop."

"Quit bein' ornery."

"Ohmigod, you can*not* speak to me that way!"

"We'll talk in the truck."

Arriving at his truck, he virtually threw me into the cab before jogging to the driver's side and closing himself in with me. I debated escaping while we had distance, but in the end, I knew he'd just catch me if I ran, so I secured my seatbelt and stared out the window.

"What the *hell* are you doing sneaking out of the convent, Lex?" he bellowed.

"How the *hell* do you know I sneaked out?" I countered, and then raised my hand. "No, never mind, this is none of your business. I don't want to know."

"Everything you do is my business…don't ever doubt it."

"It most certainly is not, you male chauvinist, lying, piece of—"

"You gonna answer my question?"

"Nope." I crossed my arms with a huff.

He swore and headed out of the parking lot.

"Where's Cameron?" I asked after a few minutes of awkward silence. "*He's* my handler. How did you even get here?"

"Cam's not available."

"Why isn't he available?"

"I'll explain when we get you safe," Reese said.

"What do you mean everything I do is your business?" I asked, once my heart calmed down a little. "I stopped being your business seven years, eleven months, and twenty-eight days ago."

"But who's counting?" Reese retorted.

I pressed my lips together to keep from screaming like a banshee and looked out the window again. I didn't remember him irritating me like that. Ever.

We continued to drive, but it didn't take me long to figure out we weren't heading toward the Convent. "Reese?"

"Yeah, Freckles?" he said, all sweet and crap.

Reese Alden wasn't sweet. Even when he was, he wasn't.

"No!" I snapped. "You don't get to call me that."

"No?"

"No." I frowned. "Where are we going?"

"Somewhere we can talk."

"I don't want to talk to you."

"Too bad," he said. "It's past time, Lex."

"Ohmigod, you don't get to make blanket decisions for me! I didn't like it when we were teenagers and I don't like it now."

"Frec—"

"No. You're not hearing me. I mean it, Reese. You don't get to do that. Take me back to the convent."

"You're not even gonna hear me out?" he asked, his tone incredulous.

"I haven't heard from you for eight years, *after* you took my virginity and my self-respect, so no, I'm *not* going to hear you out."

Reese scowled and flipped a U-turn, heading back to the convent. We sat in stony silence the rest of the way, and when we arrived at the private entrance at the back of the abbey, I slid out of the cab without comment and rushed inside.

He followed.

I scowled. "Stop following me."

"Wanna make sure you're safe."

"I'm safe. You can go."

He gave me his signature sexy grin and closed the door behind us. "Gonna make extra sure."

"I'm going to my room."

"I'll walk you."

Before I could protest, or, you know, kick him in the shins and run, our Reverend Mother came rushing toward me. “Sister Maria,” she admonished. “You know men aren’t allowed in the Abbey.”

I crossed my arms and raised an eyebrow at Reese. “I know, but he won’t leave.”

“Reese, you must go,” she ordered.

“You know him?” I squeaked.

“Yes, dear. My niece is married to Reese’s friend, Ryder.”

“Sadie’s married to Ryder Carsen?”

Now it was Reese’s turn to cross his arms. “Yep.”

I’d met Sadie a few times when I’d come to “hide” here, but never had there been any indication that her man was the same Ryder attached to Reese. I suppose I could have asked, but honestly, what were the odds?

Everything was starting to come into focus.

Horror movie, Jason’s at the glass slider, kind of focus.

“You set this up,” I whispered. “You sonofa—”

The Reverend Mother glanced at me sternly and I stopped myself.

“I don’t know how you did it, but you’re behind this somehow,” I accused.

“Indirectly,” he said.

“Have you known I was here”—I pointed to the floor, indicating the abbey—“all this time?”

“Yeah.”

Okay, this pissed me off. Irrational, maybe, but he’d known I was here, then blindsided me at the jail…no. “Reverend Mother, would you please make sure I never see this man again?”

“I…ah…I’m not sure I can do that, dear. Reese is taking over Cameron’s duties.”

“What?” I squeaked.

“I’m your new handler,” he said, a smug look on

his face. "I'll be checking on you from now until the trial."

"No. I don't accept. I'll go home before I'm subjected to having to see you every day."

"Don't be melodramatic, Lex."

I fisted my hands at my sides. "Find someone else, Reese. I'm serious."

"Not gonna happen."

I tore the veil off my head and rubbed my temples. "Then I'm done. I won't testify. I'll go home and take my chances—"

"Are you high?" Reese bellowed, making Mother jump. "You and I are gonna have a conversation, Lex, and you give me any grief, I'll take you somewhere no one'll find you."

"You will *not* threaten her that way," Mother snapped.

"He'd never hurt me," I rushed to say, which might not have been the right thing to say. One: (technically) I didn't know him anymore, so I could be wrong. But for whatever reason, I knew in my heart he'd never hurt me…at least physically. Two: I wanted him to go away, I shouldn't be defending him.

"I'd rather cut off my arm," Reese confirmed.

"*But*"—I pointed out—"after what I've been through over the past few months, maybe threatening to kidnap me might be a little melodramatic."

"You will apologize to Alexa, Reese, or you'll leave and not come back until you do," Mother ordered.

Reese rubbed the bridge of his nose and took several deep breaths. "I apologize."

"Look at her when you say it."

I bit back a smirk and waited. Reese studied me

for a few seconds and then shook his head. "I'm sorry if I scared you...," he gave me a slow smile, "Freckles."

He just *had* to throw in 'Freckles.' "I don't accept."

"Alexa!" Mother admonished. "He's apologized, you must accept."

This time, Reese smirked and I studied him for a few seconds. "*Fine*," I huffed. "Apology accepted."

"I'm sorry, Reese, but you cannot be here," Mother said. "No men in the Abbey. If you'd like to meet in the church, you are welcome to, but not here."

"Will you give me fifteen minutes, Lex?" Reese asked, his tone pinched but polite.

Would I? I wasn't sure. I'd missed him. I still missed him. He'd been my first love...he'd been my first everything, and I hadn't had a serious relationship since. Hell, I hadn't had a relationship, period. Had he dated...or hooked up with other women? No, I didn't want to know. Gah, maybe he'd had a hundred. That thought raised a streak of jealousy in me I hadn't expected. I wasn't over him. Not that that fact surprised me. Paisley had mentioned it more than once or twice (or a million) times over the last eight years.

"Fifteen minutes," he repeated.

"Fifteen minutes," I agreed. "Not a second more."

Alexa

I LED REESE through the side hallway and into the main cathedral. We took a seat facing each other in the first pew and I took a steadying breath.

Reese said nothing. Not one word. For several agonizing minutes.

I glanced at my watch. "You've got about twelve minutes left. Better start talkin'."

"Brick's dead."

Brick was Reese's father and the definition of evil. He'd been horribly abusive to Reese as a child, and his reasons were just as twisted as his actions. Brick would say Reese was the son of the devil any time Reese would disobey him, or do anything that angered him in the slightest. He would say it was proof his mother slept with other men, as Reese obviously wasn't his son, and since she was a whore, he was the son of Satan, and therefore should be treated as such.

I'm pretty sure Reese had never told that story to anyone outside of me…he'd told me as much, and one thing I knew about Reese was that he wasn't a liar. He was a lot of things, but liar wasn't one.

"Wow," I breathed out. "I'm sorry."

"Don't be sorry, Lex, he was a bastard."

This was true. He was horrible. But, still, he was Reese's father, so that had to be a bit of a mind bend. "Okay, so he's gone," I encouraged. "Why are you wasting your fifteen minutes telling me this?"

"Because it changes everything."

"What does it change?"

"This." He waved his hand between the two of us.

"I'm not following," I said. And I really wasn't. I had no idea what he was trying to tell me by osmosis and charades.

"Us."

Us? I blinked. He couldn't mean "us" as a couple. "Us" had gone up in a puff of exhaust when the sexy bastard had left me.

"Freckles?" he asked, leaning forward.

This time the nickname squeezed my heart until I thought it would pop. My eyes burned with a rush of unshed tears as a stupid little glimmer of hope popped into my idiotic brain. *Us?*

"Wha—" my voice cracked. I cleared my throat and tried again. "What exactly do you expect to happen between you and me?"

"We can start again."

My mouth dropped open of its own accord and I stared at him wondering what planet he'd fallen from.

Start again? The asshole had ripped my heart out of my chest and stomped all over it with his sexy-ass motorcycle boots. There was no starting again.

"Maybe not start again," he clarified. "I know I can't pretend the breakup and the past eight years didn't happen, but maybe we can—"

I laughed. I couldn't help it. The idea of me and Reese together again…I glanced at his hands. They were rough and calloused from working on his bike, just like I remembered. They used to roam my body, bringing me to levels of ecstasy I hadn't experienced since. Just thinking about the pleasure those magical hands could bring me warmed my cheeks and set fire to other parts of my body. My laughter fell apart, dying deep in my throat.

"Are you okay?" Reese asked.

Stupid question. "No, I'm not okay," I snapped and stood to my feet. "Nothing is okay. I *was* okay. I mean as okay as I could possibly be while tucked away in an abbey waiting to testify against someone who wants me dead, but I was surviving. Then you show up talking all this crap about starting again? How the hell am I supposed to process this?"

He stood and reached for me. I shied away, as if his touch would burn me. I wasn't afraid of Reese, but I was terrified of what I'd do as soon as those magical hands touched me. Would I jump on him, wrap my legs around his waist and attack his neck? No. The bastard broke my heart. I should be attacking him with my fists, not my…

He smiled. "Freckles—"

Ohmigod why did he have to be so hot? More heat rushed to my cheeks. What the hell was with that smile? Could he read my thoughts?

"Don't call me that. You lost that right when you—" I hiccupped.

My hiccups turned into frustrated tears and wracking sobs that I couldn't seem to stop.

"Fuck, baby, don't cry," he said, and reached for me again.

I stood so quickly I almost tripped over the pew. "I'm fine," I said, wiping away the moisture from my cheeks. "Don't *touch* me."

But my god, those hands. I wanted him to touch me.

After another sexy smile, Reese pulled me into his arms, holding me tight. He released my hair from its tie, running his fingers through my long, blonde tresses as I sobbed into his chest. He smelled like leather and soap with a hint of the cologne I'd bought him for his nineteenth birthday. His scent short-circuited my brain, and when he lifted my chin I stared at his perfect lips, wondering what it would be like to kiss them. Would he taste the same?

And when he leaves me again, will it destroy me this time?

That single rational thought hit me like a bucket of ice, making me push Reese away. I dropped my hands to my sides, smoothing out my habit as I tried not to notice the hungry look on his face. It appeared as though Reese was having as much trouble controlling his emotions as I was.

"You're right," he said, his voice deep and husky. "We can't restart when I never stopped."

"Never stopped what?" I asked.

"Missing you. Watching out for you. Loving you."

I shook my head.

No. That was too much. I couldn't process…couldn't think. I shook my head and made a mad dash for the Abbey without looking back. Once I'd closed myself into my room, I dug for the burner I had hidden behind the air vent and called Paisley. If anyone could talk me down off this ledge, it was her.

* * *

Reese

I let Alexa escape. I wasn't surprised she'd hightailed it away from me…I'd even expected it, but I'd been hopeful she might make things easy on me a little. Obviously, that hope had been misplaced. Admittedly, I was kind of glad. If she made it easy on me, she wasn't the woman I fell in love with all those years ago.

Damn, I fucked it up. All of it. But I didn't think I'd change anything. My sperm donor was a piece of shit and, if he'd known I had real feelings for Alexa, Brick would have killed her…or worse.

If I'd told Alexa the extent of all this back then, she would have gone to bat for us and probably started a war between the Spiders and the Mob. At the time, I couldn't take that chance. I may have only been nineteen, but I knew what I wanted and Alexa was everything to me. The thought of her being hurt was too much for me to fathom. I'd made the only choice I could and let her go, but I'd spent the past eight years pining for her in my own way…no one but Ryder knew anything about her…not even our crew. I had made sure of that.

Dragging my hands down my face, I left the church and headed to Ryder's. Knock me over with a feather, but I was in the mood for some of Sadie's positivity. At the very least, Ryder'd have beer.

Pulling up to the house, I wondered if I should have texted before just showing up, but as I put the truck in reverse, the front door opened, and Ryder gave me a chin lift. I parked again and climbed out.

"Sadie saw you pull up on the security cameras," Ryder said.

I nodded.

"Beer?"

"Yeah, brother, that'd be good," I said, and followed Ryder inside.

I walked into the kitchen and found Sadie pulling two beers out of the fridge. Dark hair, blue eyes, she looked a bit like Mila Kunis. Damn she was a knockout. It was hard to imagine, looking at her now, she used to be a nun. Ryder'd helped her out and he'd been a goner ever since. Lucky for him, Sadie's aunt (the current Reverend Mother of the abbey) didn't really think she was very good nun material and released her back into the world. Ryder didn't waste any time making her his.

After setting the bottles on the island, she made her way to me and pulled me in for a surprisingly strong hug. She was a little thing, but she was a great hugger.

"Hey, babe," I said.

"Hi," she breathed out. "How did it go?"

"How'd what go?"

She glanced at her husband, then back at me. "Was I not supposed to know?"

Ryder chuckled. "You weren't supposed to tell *him* you knew."

Sadie bit her lip. "Sorry, not sorry. Spill."

I filled them in on the events of the evening and Sadie's face grew sadder with every word. "She must have been so frightened," she breathed out.

I shoved down my irritation. "I never threatened her, Sadie. Why would she be afraid of me?"

"Not of you, silly goose," she said as she waved her hand dismissively. "Of thinking she was going to be thrown into jail. My word, could you imagine? Her brother's taken away to God knows where, and she's thinking she's going to get thrown into a stinky cell with strangers. After everything she's been through…"

I closed my eyes for a second. I hadn't even thought about Lex being scared…she was the strongest person I knew. Fuck! I'd gone in with my own agenda and didn't once consider she might be freaked. "Damn it," I rasped. I was an ass.

"Okay, baby," Ryder said, giving Sadie a squeeze. "Maybe lay off the guilt trip, huh?"

"Is that what I was doing?" she asked, all innocent and shit.

I took another swig of beer.

"If you love this woman as much as Ryder thinks you do," Sadie continued, "you might want to think about an apology in a big way. Like, finding out where her brother is and figuring out a way to get him safe. Show her how you feel…words don't really hold a lot of weight it sounds like."

"Sadie," Ryder warned.

"No, she's right," I ground out. "But you ever repeat that, I'll deny I ever said it."

Sadie gave me a gentle smile. "You'll figure it out, buddy. You might have to use actual words instead of grunts, but I still think you'll figure it out."

I bit back a chuckle and grunted instead.

Sadie giggled and kissed Ryder. "I'm going to curl up in our bedroom and read so you guys can talk."

"Okay, baby," he said, and kissed her again.

"Any idea where Sergei is?" Ryder asked once Sadie left us.

I shook my head. "Got a call in to Cam to find out."

"Good."

"Lex is pissed I'm her new handler."

"You expected that."

"Yeah," I said, letting out a long breath. "Wasn't expecting so much hate, though."

"She didn't move on."

"Nope." I took another swig of beer.

"Neither did you."

"Nope."

"Thought for sure after eight years, you'd be less whipped," Ryder retorted.

"Fuck you." I tipped my beer toward him. "Like you're one to talk."

Ryder laughed. "True."

My phone buzzed and I pulled it out of my pocket. "It's Cam."

Ryder nodded and leaned against the island.

"Hey, man," I said.

"Hey," Cameron said. "Got a lock on Sergei. They didn't book him. He's a C.I."

"No shit?"

"Yeah. Don't wanna go much further because I don't want to alert whoever he's informing against that I'm digging."

"Got it. I'll have the Dogs dig. Won't look weird if they do it."

The Dogs of Fire Motorcycle Club was a local club who'd taken Ryder, me, and the rest of the guys into their fold. They'd been experiencing their own issues with the Gresham Spiders and me and Ryder had been helping them deal with them with inside information.

"Good plan," Cameron said. "I'll text you what I have."

"Thanks, Cam."

"No problem."

He hung up and I was glad Ryder didn't ask for details. I'd send what Cam sent over to Booker, the Dogs resident computer whiz, and see what he could find out. I also asked him to see what he could dig up on the FBI. I was pushing my luck, I was sure, but I knew there was a mole somewhere. Someone giving the Spiders information about the women testifying, I just couldn't prove it yet, so I needed someone to go deep.

Until then, I needed to figure out a way to apologize to Alexa…in a big way.

I kept my visit short and headed home less than an hour later, letting myself into the home I'd gutted and redone with Alexa in mind. We'd probably never live here, but I'd thought of her while I was building sweat equity.

To be honest, I thought about her even when I wasn't working. She was never far from my heart and mind.

As I threw a frozen burrito into the microwave and grabbed a beer from the fridge, memories flooded my head and I took a minute to sit with them for a bit.

* * *

Alexa walked out of her office building and smiled at one of her co-workers...an older woman who appeared to be nearing retirement age. Today it was a woman, yesterday it had been some asshole whose eyes wandered too close to her tits. I watched her from across the street...had been watching her for over a week now...and as stalkerish as it might have been, now that I'd found her, I wasn't about to let her out of my sight.

She'd done it. Become a lawyer. She'd been working for Miller, Williams, and Wall for the past two years while she went through school and had just passed the Bar. I couldn't have been more proud of her, but her success drove home the fact that she'd moved on without me and that fuckin' killed me.

She'd been taken a week later…

Right in the middle of Ryder's sister's abduction, Lex had also disappeared. I hadn't known that at the time, as I was tasked with making sure Sadie was safe while Ryder worked with Cameron to get Scottie back. I didn't mind...I liked Sadie, and figured Lex was safe for the moment, but what I should have done was put one of our guys on Alexa watch.

Once Scottie was found (all the way in fuckin' Savannah, Georgia), Ryder had filled me in on everything that had gone down at the flophouse, but he'd omitted the fact that Alexa and Paisley had been held along with his sister. I didn't get that information until long after Alexa had been sequestered in the abbey.

I had been frantic, not knowing where she was,

who she was with, if she was safe. Ryder had finally told me the full story, and assured me she was safe, but refused to tell me exactly where she was. After a near fist fight with my closest friend, he'd given me Cameron's information who had reluctantly agreed to let me assist with Alexa watch.

It was in his best interest to do so, considering I had some serious computer skills and had a good relationship with Booker who could hack anyone, so if Cameron wanted me to stay out of the way, he needed to give me something to keep my woman safe.

My heart and soul felt like she was still my woman and since there was no evidence of another man in her life, I was gonna figure out a way to get her back.

Little did I know what it would take to do that…

The ding of the microwave brought me back to the present and I grabbed the food and beer and headed to my desk to do some work. I'd give Alexa some space, but not much, and I'd make it up to her…even if it killed me.

THREE

Alexa

TWO DAYS LATER, after yet another sleepless night, I dragged myself into the abbey's kitchen and poured my third cup of coffee of the morning.

"Alexa?"

I turned to find Sadie walking in, and my stomach churned. "Hi, Sadie. Everything okay?"

"You tell me," she said, and sat at the long banquet table.

"I'm not following."

"Reese—"

"No." I shook my head. "Sorry, Sadie, I don't mean to be rude, but that subject is off limits."

"I don't want to pry," she said. "Consider the subject dropped."

I relaxed. "Thanks."

"Gosh, he was distraught the other night…so worried he'd scared you." She flicked away non-existent lint off her jeans. One thing about Sadie was, she might not be a nun anymore, but she was always dressed immaculately.

I rolled my eyes, but didn't comment.

"Poor man. I was sure I saw a tear in his eye."

"Ohmigod, Reese Alden does *not* cry," I snapped.

"Maybe not, but he was pretty upset."

"You've got that Catholic guilt thing down, don't ya?" I accused.

She rose to her feet and faced me. "Look, I'm really not trying to pry. But if you ever need to talk to someone, I'm a really good listener. And Reese is a good man… which I'm sure you know. He doesn't always say the right thing, and tends to grunt instead of using real words, but I've never seen him the way he was the other night, so you must mean something to him." She sighed. "I'm sorry. I'm prying. I'll stop."

"Thanks, Sadie. I appre—"

"After I say just one more thing," she interrupted.

I squeezed my eyes shut and sipped my coffee while I tried to keep my cool.

"He feels horrible—"

"No. I'm shutting this conversation down, Sadie." I pushed away from the counter. "*Please*. You have no idea what went on with me and Reese and without my best friend to talk to, I just want to forget about all of it. No offense, but Paisley's the only one I want to talk to. Any chance of getting her here?"

Sadie bit her lip and shook her head. "I'm sorry, Alexa."

"I'm working with the kindergarteners today, so I should really get going. Take care, Sadie." I walked out of the kitchen without a backward glance. I had thirty minutes before I started my shift reading to the kids, so I escaped to my bedroom, and gave myself five minutes to melt down.

I couldn't keep doing this. I needed to find out how to separate myself from Reese once and for all. If I didn't, I'd break again, and I didn't think I could put myself back together this time around.

* * *

Reese

I walked out my front door to find Alexa's best friend, Paisley, screeching her silver Mercedes to a halt in front of me. She climbed out of her car, marched up to me, and shoved me…hard.

"What the fuck, Paisley?" I snapped.

"Stop it!" she demanded.

"Stop what?" The last time I'd seen Paisley was the day before I'd broken up with Alexa, so the fact she knew where I lived unsettled me somewhat…but she'd always been good at finding shit.

"Ohmigod, Reese, sometimes I want to shoot you." She jabbed a finger at me. "And you know what? I own a gun now, so watch your back!"

Paisley had turned her love of subterfuge into a career and now worked for the Vancouver Police Department as a detective, but not one on the street…she "found" people who typically didn't want to be found, from behind a desk.

I crossed my arms. "You wanna fill me in on what's crawled up your ass, babe? 'Cause I got shit to do and you're preventin' me from doin' it."

"You broke her!" she bellowed.

"Paisley," I ground out.

"No! You need to back off, buster. You broke her once and I won't let you do it again."

"Buster?" I smirked. "You wound me, Paisley."

"Oh, suck it, Reese. You have businesses to run. Bars to open for people to get drunk. You don't have time to 'handle' Lex."

"Ryder's got the bars covered, Paisley. My attention won't be divided."

"Regardless, Reese. You need to find someone else to handle her or I'm comin' for you."

"Not gonna happen, babe, so you better get used to the idea."

She let out a screech and came flying at me again, but this time I was prepared. I caught her and gently pinned her arms at her side.

"You can't do this to her *again*, asshole," she hissed.

"Everything okay here?"

I craned my neck to see Cullen Wallace walk out my front door. Cullen was doing some work on my house, and he just so happened to be the brother of Hatch, who was the Sergeant at Arms for the Dogs of Fire.

"All good," I said.

"He's being an asshole," Paisley hissed.

"Settle, Paisley, and I'll let you go."

"Let me go and I'm kicking you in the family jewels," she threatened.

"Noted," I said, and held her a little tighter.

She tried to wiggle away, but I had her locked in. "Let me go," she demanded.

"Feel better if you let the lady go, Reese," Cullen said, but it was more of a warning.

"You gonna calm down?" I asked Paisley.

"Yes."

"You lyin'?"

"Yes."

"Reese," Cullen warned again, and stepped toward us.

I released her and stepped out of kicking distance. "Always liked your honesty, babe."

"Well, that's good, because I'm going to cut you."

"Not a fan of your viciousness, however."

Cullen crossed his arms and Paisley studied him. "You don't have to stand there all manly and stuff, Reese would never hurt me."

I was glad she knew that, but a little surprised she admitted it out loud.

"I'm gonna go ahead and stand here 'all manly and stuff' anyway," Cullen informed her.

"You do you, BooBoo," she retorted, then turned her rage back on me. "You need to forget about her."

"No."

Tears flooded her eyes. "You really must hate her."

"How do you figure?"

"If you *ever* loved her, you'd let her go. Let her live her life."

"Paisley, I don't hate Alexa," I said, suddenly exhausted. "I'm gonna fix this. And I'm not lettin' another handler near her. No one else can protect her right…obviously. I won't let her end up in jail or on the radar of the people she's testifyin' against."

"You broke her," she repeated in a whisper, wiping a rogue tear from her face.

"Babe, I'm gonna fix it," I rasped. "I love her. Never stopped, so I'm gonna make this right."

"She won't have it."

"She will, Paisley. But when all this shit's over with the Russians…if she wants out, I'll walk away."

Paisley snorted. "That's what I'm afraid of."

"It's gonna be her choice."

She raised an eyebrow. "Then I'm gonna do whatever I can to make sure she stays strong and resists you."

"Yeah?"

"Yeah."

"So you don't want your best friend to be happy. Good to know," I deadpanned.

"See, here's the problem," she said, wagging a finger at me. "You make her miserable. She was good…really good, and then you broke her and there wasn't enough duct tape in the world that could put her back together. I can't watch her go through that again."

"Paisley, I'm gonna fix this," I said…again.

She studied me.

"You gonna make this more difficult?" I asked.

Paisley shrugged. "Maybe."

I crossed my arms again. "It'll go better if you support her in this."

"You mean, support *you*. You don't give a damn about Alexa's feelings. If you did, you wouldn't be back dragging all this crap back up."

"Enough," I ground out. "We're done with the conversation, Paisley. I gotta head out. You want to stick around and yell at my front door…or Cullen, knock yourself out."

I climbed onto my bike and took off. I saw Paisley flip me the bird in my side mirror and almost laughed. I'd hoped she wouldn't give me grief, but now that I knew what I was up against, I'd have to step up my game.

Pulling into the Dogs of Fire compound, I parked my bike and headed toward the entrance. I raised my face to the camera at the outside door and the door buzzed, so I stepped into a dimly lit hallway and made my way to another door, raising my head again. I was buzzed in and I walked inside to find Hawk waiting for me. He gave me a chin lift. "You got somethin'?"

Hawk nodded. "Follow me."

He led me down a side hallway and to a control room of sorts, waving to a chair. I dragged it to where Hawk sat in front of a computer. "I had Booker do a search and Sergei's in some deep shit."

Booker was the VP of the Dogs and a computer whiz. If you needed someone found, or their identity erased, he was the man to do it.

"Figured."

Hawk pulled up a series of photos. "Here's your FBI mole."

I leaned in. "Don't know him."

"Jaxon does," Hawk said, facing me.

Jaxon Quinn was FBI and related to a few of the Dogs. He had helped get a couple of Dogs' kids out from under Brick's thumb.

Maverick was a recruit for the Club, married to Hawk's daughter, Lily, and he and his sister had been kidnapped by Brick. That's how Brick had met his maker. I wasn't entirely sure who killed him, but honestly, I didn't care.

"Once Jaxon and his team knew who Sergei was informin' to, they dug deeper. His "handler" is Sean May and he's a Spider."

“I doubt that,” I countered. “I know all the Spiders.”

Hawk shook his head. “You know Crystal?”

“Yeah.”

Crystal was Shovelhead’s old lady and had been a club whore before that.

“It’s her son,” he said.

“Shit, seriously?” I breathed out.

Hawk nodded.

“This feels eerily like sleeper agent type shit,” I said.

“Agreed.”

“So Crystal groomed her kid to get into the FBI and work for the Spiders within the system?” I asked, sitting back.

“I think it’s more likely he made the FBI and she has somethin’ on him…or the Spiders do, and they’ve used that to their advantage.”

“Shit,” I hissed.

Crystal had fooled us. Admittedly, she was never really on our radar, but from what I could remember when it came to Crystal, she was either drunk, high, or both and not the sharpest tool in the shed. Apparently, she was smarter than anyone realized.

“Jaxon’s reading Cameron Shane in on this,” Hawk said.

I nodded. “Okay.”

“We’re gonna figure out how to get Sergei out. It won’t touch Alexa.”

“’Preciate it, brother.” I stood. “Keep me posted?”

“Yeah, man. No problem.”

I nodded and headed out of the compound.

Alexa

I'D MADE IT through the day without further incident and was looking forward to hanging with my other "refugees." There were eleven of us being hidden from the Spiders and the Mob. We were all dressed in nun habits and trying our best to fake being Catholic (some better than others…well, better than me anyway). The youngest victim, Molly, was actually being fostered by the Reverend Mother, so she simply got a new name…no costume required. I found out that another material witness was among the women being held at the crack house, and she and I had become fast friends, especially when we started swapping stories.

Summer and I were in the chapel just off the main cathedral, setting up for a youth service beginning in a couple of hours and discussing some of the specifics of our predicaments.

"I can't believe Bogdan Romanov was your father," Summer said, her voice sounding slightly awed. "I never met him personally…just heard rumors."

I sighed. "Most of the rumors you heard were probably true. Believe it or not, he was really good as a dad. As a man, not so much."

Summer nodded. "Murdering countless people kind of makes that impossible. No offense."

"None taken." I was still working out my feelings toward my father. The disconnect between the man I knew as "Papa," and the man who got rid of people who threatened him, real or perceived, was narrowing. I wasn't so delusional to think my father was perfect, but I also loved him and nothing he did would change that. My question was, how did you continue to justify loving someone so evil? I still didn't have that answer. "How long did you work for Mr. Markell?"

Tony Markell had been the "family's" accountant and as crooked as they came. I had a feeling Summer had been hired not because of her skill-set (although, she seemed quite intelligent), but because of her looks. She was exotically beautiful with a Maggie Q quality about her.

Before Summer could answer my question, however, a surprise guest walked into the chapel. "Sisters," Cameron said.

"Agent Shane," Summer said, her smile quick and her cheeks pinkening.

"Hi, Cameron."

"Summer, would you mind giving me and Lex a minute?" he asked.

"Of course," she said, and gave me a questioning look as she walked out of the chapel.

"I'm not speaking to you," I grumbled.

He chuckled. "I figured."

I crossed my arms. "*Why* didn't you tell me?"

"About letting Reese take over or that I had someone watching you?"

"Both," I said.

He waved to a pew and we sat facing each other. "I got stuck on somethin' and should have put someone a little more senior on watch Alexa duty."

"You don't really call it 'watch Alexa duty,' do you?"

Cameron smiled. "No, but we probably should."

"Sergei—"

"Was in trouble. I get it."

"But why Reese?" I whispered. "You must know our history."

"Didn't have a choice, Lex. He's been in this since pretty early on."

"What?" I squeaked.

He sighed. "Thought that'd be less of a surprise."

"I haven't seen him in eight years, Cameron. How would he even know where I was?"

"Ryder."

"Wait," I said, trying to wrap my head around everything he was saying. "How would Ryder know?"

"His sister was being held in the same place you were."

"She was in Savannah?"

"Yeah."

"Ohmigod," I breathed out. "How did I miss that?"

Paisley and I had both been drugged for days, so

we didn't realize we were in Savannah until we were rescued by the FBI. Then it was a day or two of debriefing before finally being allowed to come home…well, to the abbey.

"Outside of the fact you and Scottie were separated? Ryder didn't want you to know, Lex." He squeezed my arm. "But when Reese found out, it took all of Ryder's efforts to keep him from getting involved."

"Yeah, that sounds like Reese," I conceded.

"What the hell is going on here?" Reese's angry voice echoed through the room.

I glanced up to see him stalking toward us. My stomach flipped. He must have snuck in through the tunnels. There were secret passageways throughout Portland, believed to have once been used during Prohibition, and the church had utilized them when we'd been snuck in.

I focused back on Reese. Lordy, he looked edible. Dark jeans, motorcycle boots, and a ribbed, long-sleeved shirt stretched taut over his muscular chest.

"Hey, Reese." Cameron smiled, slowly rising to his feet as though the fact a very angry ex-biker wasn't walking toward him looking like he was itching to murder him.

"What the fuck are you doin' here, Cameron?"

"Filling Lex in," Cameron said.

"That didn't answer my question," he seethed.

"What do you want, Reese?" I asked.

"I need a moment of your time, *sister*," Reese said, still glaring at Cameron.

"Well, as you can see, I'm busy," I said.

"I was just leaving," Cameron said. "I'm gonna be out of pocket for a little while, Lex, but if you need me, or Reese can't help you with something, leave me a message and I'll call you back as soon as I can."

"She won't need you," Reese snapped.

"Can you kill someone and not get caught?" I asked, and scowled up at Reese. "I might need you to take care of a six-foot-two rat."

Cameron chuckled. "Well, I'll let you two talk."

"No, it's okay," I argued. "You can take him with you."

Cameron leaned down and kissed my cheek. "I'll see you in a few weeks."

The six-foot-two rat forced his way between us, and Cameron smirked before walking out the way he came.

"Just how close have you two become?" Reese snapped.

"Excuse me?"

"I didn't stutter."

"He's my *handler*."

"No. *I'm* your handler."

"You are unbelievable!" I snapped.

"We can talk about this in private."

"No."

"Lex."

"No," I repeated. "You don't get to walk in here and stomp your jealous little foot and then demand we speak."

He sighed. "Baby."

"Oh, hell no," I snapped.

Reese ignored my anger and waved me toward one of the offices in the back. "Shall we?"

I wrinkled my nose, but reluctantly led him out of the chapel. Reese laid his hand on my lower back and gave me a gentle push when I hesitated at the door, then closed us in.

I put distance between us and crossed my arms. “What’s up?”

He smiled slowly and leaned against the closed door. “I wanted to give you an update.”

“Cameron just gave me the low-down.”

“Not about that.”

I gasped. “You’ve found Sergei?”

“No…,” he said, but then added, “well, yes…sort of.”

“What do you mean, ‘no, well, yes, sort of’?” I demanded.

“We know who the mole is and who’s pulling Sergei’s strings, so the Dogs have a plan to get him out without it touching you.”

“What plan?”

“Can’t share that—”

“Why can’t you share it?” I snapped, throwing my hands in the air. “Gah! This is so like you. You refuse to share anything with me!”

“I *can’t* share with you, ’cause I don’t know the plan.”

“Then why are you here if you can’t tell me anything?”

He grinned. Slowly. Sexily.

Dick!

“I’m here because I promised I’d keep you in the loop with information when I had it,” he said. “I wish I had more.”

“I bet Cameron would know.”

Reese hissed out a rather vulgar curse.

I shrugged. “Well, he would.”

“Doesn’t mean he’d tell you.”

“Maybe not,” I conceded.

Reese sighed. "Sergei's gettin' out, baby, and being watched until he does, so I figured you'd want to know."

I nodded. "I would…I do."

"Good."

I crossed my arms. "Don't you have a job?"

"I have many business interests. I own bars and some commercial properties…Ryder's lookin' out for them so I can be with you."

"Sounds pretty convenient."

"Just brothers who have each others' backs." He studied me. "You doin' okay?"

"Golden."

He sighed. "Lex."

"What, Reese?" I made my tone as acidy as possible.

He continued to study me and I dropped my head to stare at the floor. I'd counted the pattern on the carpet twice before the toe of his boots appeared in my view. I raised my head to find him standing very close…too close. I tried to step back, but a large, wooden desk stopped me. "What are you doing?" I whispered.

"Makin' sure you're okay."

"I told you. I'm golden," I repeated.

His hand slid to my jaw and his thumb gently brushed my cheek. "You're lying."

"I am not."

"You know how I know?"

"Oh, please, handsome, enlighten me," I deadpanned.

"You have a dancing freckle."

I pulled away from his fingers. "Ohmigod, Reese, freckles don't dance."

"Yours does." He touched my cheek again gently. "But only when you lie."

"You're demented."

"Talk to me, Lex."

"About what exactly?" I challenged.

"Anything. Everything."

I shook my head.

"Did you forget I'm a good listener?"

"You're a *terrible* listener," I countered, and realized this had been his ploy all along. "But you've probably changed since then." I squared my shoulders. "I have."

"Yeah?"

"Yes."

"You still do this little thing with your nose when you're irritated with me."

My hand flew to my nose of its own accord. "What thing?"

"It flares a little…like a rabbit."

I let out a snort of derision and lowered my hand. "It does not."

He leaned in and kissed my nose quickly. "It so does."

"Move away."

"How ya doin'?"

"I'm super, handsome. How 'bout you?"

"I'm good now, baby."

"Well, that's fabulous." I pushed on his waist to try and get him to move away. He didn't budge.

"Lex."

"What?" I snapped. "Will you just *move*, please?"

"How are you really doin'?"

I rolled my eyes. "If I say I'm terrible, will you go away?"

"Nope."

"If I say I'm great, will you go away?"

He smiled. "Nope."

"Didn't think so," I said with a sigh.

"So…" He backed me up against the desk again. "How are you really doin'?"

"How do you think I am?"

"I think you're holdin' it together with duct tape and dental floss…MacGyver style."

I bit back a smile.

He stroked my cheek. "Am I close?"

I shrugged.

"What can I do?" he asked.

"Nothing."

He cocked his head. "At all?"

"You could go."

"Other than that."

"Then, no."

"Not even ribeye from the Q?" he challenged.

Like Pavlov's dog, my mouth began to water. "You brought ribeye from the Q?"

"Nope, but I could make a run. We could have dinner together."

I shook my head, even though all I wanted right now was ribeye from the Q. Damn him and his sorcerer's tongue.

"No?" he pressed.

I shook my head again.

"Not even ribeye *and* tiramisu?"

I licked my lips and swallowed, forcing myself to shake my head.

"How long as has it been since you had all of that and a glass of merlot?"

"How could you possibly know I like merlot? I

didn't drink—" I let out a frustrated squeak. "No, don't tell me. I don't want to know."

"I'm going to pick up food and I'll be back at six. We'll have dinner."

"Reese—"

His mouth landed on mine and I gasped, which gave him better access so he could deepen the kiss. Good God, I'd missed this. I gripped his shirt and leaned into him; hardly noticing that he'd tugged off my veil and released my hair from its tie.

Reese broke the kiss and ran his thumb over my bottom lip. "Missed this, baby."

"Maybe you'd get more if you stopped acting like a jealous douchebag."

He raised an eyebrow in silent admonishment.

"I don't know what you want from me, Reese," I hissed. "This is emotional blackmail and it's not fair."

"I'm not tryin' to put one over on you, Lex."

"No?"

"No, baby. Fuck!" He squeezed his eyes shut for a second. "Look. This whole situation is shit. I didn't think it would take me as long as it did to get shot of the sperm donor. By the time I felt it was safe for you, there was all that shit with your dad."

"What shit?" I asked.

"The hit on him and the RICO shit with your brother."

"What RICO shit with my brother?"

"Your brother's helping to build a RICO case against the guys who killed your dad."

"What?" I bellowed.

"What did you think he was doing?"

"Not *that*! Ohmigod, Reese, they're going to kill him." I shoved him. "Move please. I need space."

He released me and stepped to the door so I could pace.

"He's covered, Lex. Hawk's makin' sure. The Dogs are watchin' him."

I dragged my hands through my hair. "You have a bird 'making sure'? And why are dogs watching Sergei?"

Reese smiled. "Hawk's an officer in the Dogs of Fire MC. They've got guys watchin' Sergei and they have a contact with the FBI who is going inside. It won't be weird for him to be there."

I crossed my arms. "Who is this FBI person? Do you trust him?"

"I haven't met him, but I trust Cameron, so by extension, I trust him."

"So Cameron set it up?" I asked.

"Yeah."

"How did you wiggle your way into being my handler?"

He sighed. "The day you snuck out, Cam had been pulled from your case to another one more pressing...his specialty is kidnap and ransom recovery, and they needed him there. If he'd been on shift, you would have never gotten out."

"You don't think?"

"Oh, I *know*, baby. And so does he."

I wrinkled my nose, but didn't disagree. Cameron always seemed to know what I was doing before I did it, but he never got angry with me if I tried to press the limits of my "protection." Hence, his little talk with me earlier. He was always kind when delivering bad news.

"Jaxon Quinn is FBI and the brother of a couple of the Dogs of Fire members. He deputized me and

Ryder so that he can call on us when needed. But it really only happened because I wasn't lettin' anyone else near you."

"Really," I droned. "The FBI 'made' you a deputy because you demanded it. If that's the case, then the FBI isn't quite the powerhouse it makes itself out to be, is it?"

Reese chuckled. "It's a little more complicated than that, but it's essentially a one-woman dispensation."

"So, let me get this straight. The FBI gave you special "dispensation" so that you could make sure I was safe."

"Yes."

The tears I'd been fighting back slipped out and I dropped my head again, but Reese closed the distance between us again, lifting my face and wiping them away.

"I'm gonna fix this," he whispered.

"I don't think you can."

"You gonna let me try?"

I bit my lip, staring up at him. Was I going to let him try? I didn't know if I *could* let him in again.

If I took Paisley's advice, I'd never see him again. But if I listened to my heart, I'd have the chance of seeing him every day for the rest of my life…or risk the chance of my heart being broken again. But, damn it. I wanted him back. All of him. His quirks, his vices, his sweetness…all of it.

I nodded and he kissed me again, pulling me closer. "I thought you'd make this harder," he admitted.

"I can."

He chuckled. "No, I'm good."

I squeezed my eyes shut. "Don't break me again, okay?"

"Look at me." I met his eyes and he stroked my cheek. "I love you, Alexa. That hasn't changed. I wish I could say that if I had it to do all over again I'd do things differently, but I wouldn't. My number one priority in everything I do is protecting you and I won't apologize for that."

I scowled, leaning away from his touch. "Wrong thing to say to me, Reese."

"But it's the truth. If I hadn't done what I did, you'd be dead and I wouldn't have been able to deal with it."

"I wouldn't be dead, Reese."

"I wasn't willing to take that chance."

"But you didn't let me weigh in on that," I countered. "I won't do that again with you. We either start off as partners or not at all."

He studied me, then his stupid mouth went up into a slow, stupid smile.

"What?" I snapped.

Reese chuckled. "I'm in."

"Oh. Good."

He grinned again.

"Why do you keep looking at me like that?"

"Because you just made me a commitment."

I raised an eyebrow. "Oh is that what you heard?"

"You bet your ass it is," he said, leaning down to kiss me gently. "I love you, Alexa Romanov and from this second on, you're mine."

"I was yours before."

"Yeah, but this time, I'm not lettin' you go."

"How can I trust that?"

"Well, first, I said it and I don't lie…second, Paisley already threatened to cut my dick off, so—"

I gasped. "What?"

He filled me in on the story and I covered my mouth with my hand in an effort to hide my mirth. Reese grinned. "It was pretty funny."

"She was defending my honor," I said. "You should be scared."

"The day five-foot-four, one-hundred-thirty pounds soaking wet, Paisley Bell scares me, I will probably be dead."

"Well, you should at least feign fear."

"Ya think?"

I nodded. "Especially since she's the one who picked up the pieces after you broke me."

He sighed. "How long am I'm gonna have to suffer for that?"

"For as long as we've been apart."

"Eight years?"

"And a day."

Reese rolled his eyes. "We'll have to work on that."

"You're gonna be working on a lot of things, buddy."

"Yeah?" I nodded. He stepped closer to me again. "But we'll be together."

I bit my lip and nodded again. "We'll be together. But I reserve the right to make your life hell on occasion."

"Fuck me, I love you."

"Well, fuck me, I love you, too."

He slid his hands to my neck. "You know what it does to me when your sweet mouth utters filthy words."

I shivered. "I remember."

"Don't do it again unless you expect me to do something about it."

"What if I want you to do something about it?" I challenged.

"Not fucking you in a church, Alexa."

I wrinkled my nose. "Well, that's stupid."

"You frustrated, Freckles?"

I squeezed my legs together. "Yes," I whispered.

He locked the door and pushed me against the desk, running his lips across my neck as he lifted my habit. His hand slid under the waistband of my panties and between my legs. "So wet."

"Little backed up, Reese," I rasped.

"I'm gonna take care of that, baby."

Before I could comment, he tore my underwear from my body and shoved the shredded lace into his jeans pocket.

"What are you doing?" I asked.

He grinned. "Already told you."

"*With* my panties?" I clarified.

"I'm keeping those," he said as his hand went back between my legs. "Now, shush."

His thumb went to my clit and I shushed. Kneeling in front of me, he disappeared under my habit and his mouth replaced his hand.

"Ohmigod," I groaned out.

As his tongue slid along my clit, my knees started to buckle, but Reese lifted me onto the desk and guided my legs over his shoulders. "Shh, baby. You need to be quiet," he warned in a whisper.

I bit my lip and nodded, and he went back to his task. This time, he sucked my clit as he slid two fingers inside of me and I almost came apart right then, but Reese still knew me and my body, and adjusted in an effort to make me squirm…literally. “Reese,” I hissed.

Keeping his hand between my legs, he shifted so I’d have to wrap my legs around his waist, and leaned over to kiss me. He continued to work my pussy with an expertise that always amazed me, and as my climax hit, his mouth covered mine again and he kissed me as I whimpered.

I gripped his biceps and kissed him back with a desperation I hadn’t felt in a long time. Reese smiled against my lips and helped me sit up. “Better?” he asked.

I nodded and he ran his tongue over one of his fingers.

“Still taste like honey, Lex.”

I squirmed again. “Don’t make this harder.”

“Don’t think that’s possible.”

I ran my hand over his rock-hard cock. “Let me return the favor.”

“No.”

“What?” Reese Alden *never* turned down a blow job. Ever.

He kissed me again. “Until I have all night to show you exactly how I feel about you, I’ll suffer.”

I couldn’t help but shiver again as I let my habit fall back to my ankles. “And when will this all-night thing happen, exactly?”

“As soon as it’s safe.”

“That could be forever.”

“It won’t be forever,” he promised.

“Tonight?”

He chuckled. “No, but soon, baby.”

I scooped my hair back into its tie and Reese

helped me with my veil. "Are you still bringing me dinner?"

"Of course I'm still bringing you dinner."

"Are you really not giving me back my panties?"

"Nope." He kissed my nose. "And if you don't replace 'em, I'll make it worth your while tonight."

"As much as I appreciate the modicum of relief you provided, honey, if you're suffering, I'm suffering."

"Yeah?"

I nodded.

"Then I better make a plan, huh?"

I nodded again. "Definitely."

"I'll take care of it."

I wrapped my arms around his waist. "Do you really have to go?"

"I do."

I felt my veil slide off my head again, and I groaned. "Reese. Why do you keep doing that?"

"Because kissing a nun creeps me the fuck out, Lex. Even if it's you."

I snatched it from his hand. "Do you know how long it takes me to put that thing back on?"

"The plan is you won't have to wear it for much longer."

"I don't testify for six months." I slid the veil back on and Reese helped me fix it.

"Yeah, well you're not stayin' here for six months."

"Don't get my hopes up, sugar bear."

Reese let out a quiet grunt and my veil was off my head again as he pulled me close and kissed me deeply.

I broke the kiss and raised an eyebrow. "What the

heck was that?"

He kissed me again and I slid my arms around his waist.

"Fuckin' sugar bear, baby. Gets me every time."

I giggled. "I thought you hated it."

He smirked. "Never said I hated it."

I smacked his chest playfully. "You led me to believe you did."

"Did I?"

I rolled my eyes. "Crazy man."

He grinned and helped me with my veil again.

"I should get going," he said.

I sighed. "Probably."

He smiled. "I'm gonna be back in a couple hours, Lex. Don't cry."

"Oh, suck it, big man. I'm going to use the next two hours to plan your demise."

"Make sure it has somethin' to do with dying while fuckin' you, yeah?"

"Sure, sure. But only after I come. You might die frustrated, but I will have finished nicely."

He dropped his head back and laughed. "Damn I've missed you."

I jabbed a finger into his chest. "Then, don't leave again."

He raised my hand to his mouth and kissed my palm. "Rather have my dick cut off by Paisley."

I wrinkled my nose. "Well, that's a visual I'd rather not have."

He kissed me again. "I'll see you at six."

I nodded and followed him out of the office. The chapel was still empty, so I headed back into the abbey and Reese headed for the tunnels.

Alexa

SIX O'CLOCK ROLLED around and Reese hadn't arrived yet. If he was anyone else, I wouldn't be concerned, but I could always set my watch to Reese. He was never late. I didn't even have a way to contact him, so my panic was on overdrive.

I paced my room, but quickly realized he wouldn't be allowed back here, so I headed out into the hallway and made my way to the chapel. As I walked inside, a strong arm snaked around my waist and I let out a squeak.

"It's me, Freckles," Reese whispered, and I turned to face him. "Where have you been?"

I leaned up and kissed him quickly. "Well, I was freaking out in my room, but then I realized you couldn't come to me, so I came here."

"Why were you freaking out?"

"You were late."

"Wasn't late."

I rolled my eyes. "Well, duh. I figured that out, which is why I'm here."

He chuckled. "You hungry?"

"Starving." I cupped him over his jeans.

"For food, baby."

I giggled. "Yes, for that too."

He nodded toward the exit of the chapel. "Reverend Mother said we could use an office back there."

I blushed. "Oh, really?"

He grinned. "Come on. Everything's ready."

He took my hand and led me through the back of the chapel and into a private room, locking the door behind us. The space had been transformed. He'd lit candles, set a romantic table including wine glasses, and the food smelled delicious.

"Aw," I cooed.

"You like?"

"I love it, sugar bear." I slid my arms around his waist. "Thank you."

He grinned, leaning down to kiss me again and removing my veil. "You're welcome."

"How are you getting in and out of here?" I asked as we sat down to eat.

"Tunnels."

"I know *that*, but aren't you worried someone will follow you?"

"I've got it covered."

"Reese, don't be flippant about this."

"I'm not. Ryder and I have it covered."

I sighed. "What does that mean?"

"Plausible deniability."

This was the same shit he used to say when he didn't want me to know what he was doing. "You know what?" I snapped. "I still hate plausible deniability."

"Well, you're gonna have to deal with it, Lex," he said grabbing a fork. "Because you're not gettin' more."

"Remember when I said I'll only accept a partnership?"

"Yeah, I remember."

I gave him a pointed look.

He grinned. "Still not gonna happen."

I let out a frustrated grunt. "Then I'm done."

"No you're not."

"Reese," I hissed. "You do—"

"Remember when I told you my biggest priority in life was to keep you safe?" he challenged, interrupting my tirade.

"I *am* safe. You're the one who's risking your life."

He cocked his head and studied me. "Do you really think I'm that stupid?"

"I don't think you want me to answer that," I said, and took a bite of steak.

Before I could take another bite, Reese rose to his feet, took my knife and fork out of my hand, and leaned down to get face-to-face with me. "You bein' feisty, Freckles?"

I swallowed. "If I say no?"

"Then you're insultin' me."

I did *not* want him to think I was insulting him. That wouldn't go well for me, yet, I still couldn't resist messing with him. "Um…"

"Alexa," he growled.

I bit back a smile. "I'm being feisty."

"What happens when you get feisty, baby?"

I licked my lips and asked hopefully, "I get spanked?"

He chuckled. "No, Lex, that's *not* what happens."

"Yes, it is!" I rushed to say. Oh, God, please, let it be yes.

"Are you trying to get to dessert before you've finished dinner?" he challenged.

"If it involves your hand on my butt, yes, yes I am."

He kissed me gently and far too quickly. "Let's see how the night progresses, hmm?" He sat back down and smoothed his paper napkin across his lap as though it were the finest linen.

"Reese?"

"Yes, Lex?"

I narrowed my eyes. "What are you doing?"

He used his fork to point to his dinner. "I'm eating, baby."

"Don't you 'baby' me, sugar bear."

He grinned. "You need some relief, Lex?"

I squirmed. "Nope."

"You sure?"

I squeezed my legs together. "Yep. I'm great."

"Did you wear panties?"

"Yes," I lied.

He chuckled. "No you didn't."

"You were very adamant about not fucking me in a church, Reese"—I jabbed my fork at him—"so this is on you, bub."

He gave me a sexy sideways smile. "We're not in the church, Lex."

I choked on my sip of wine and set the glass down. "What?" I squeaked.

"So, I'll ask you again," he said…slowly. "Are you wearing panties?"

"That depends…"

"On?"

"Whether or not there will be spanking," I challenged.

He leaned forward and raised an eyebrow. "If I guarantee my hand will connect with your ass at some point tonight?"

I sat back and licked my lips. "Then, Mr. Alden, I'm panty-less."

"Show me."

"Show you?"

"Hmm-mm."

I grinned and rose to my feet, unzipping my habit, sliding it over my shoulders, and letting it pool at my feet. I was completely naked underneath.

"Fuck me," Reese breathed out and stood.

I threw my hands in the air. "I have been *trying* to!"

He smiled gently. "Wasn't gonna fuck you in that getup."

"Ohmigod, Reese, I'm the same person. I'm not a nun. Think of it as a costume."

Reese shook his head. "Wouldn't fuck you in a nun costume either."

"Well, there go my Halloween plans." Of course, I said this still standing naked in front of him while he stared at me.

"You've gained weight."

I suddenly felt really self-conscious. "Forget it."

"Lex," he whispered.

"What?" I snapped, bending to reach for my discarded habit.

He closed the distance between us and yanked the fabric from my hands. "Don't."

I tried to cover myself. "You just called me fat."

"No, I didn't," he corrected, moving my hands behind my back. "I just mentioned you've gained weight. I like it…love it, actually. Fuck, baby, you were always gorgeous, but now you're even more of a knockout."

"Are you sure?"

Taking my hand, Reese placed it over his cock. "Does this feel sure?"

He was rock hard. "You appear to have gained a little weight too."

He grinned and covered my mouth with his, sliding his arm around my waist as he pulled me close and slipped his hand between my legs. I whimpered with need, but he rewarded me by sliding two fingers inside of me and working my clit with his thumb.

"Soaked, baby," he rasped, and I nodded.

I gripped his shirt. "Don't stop."

"I'm not stoppin', baby." He kissed me quickly and grabbed his phone to put on some music. "To muffle your screams," he explained.

"You're so sure I'm going to scream?" I challenged.

I was met with a raised eyebrow as he removed his clothes.

His cock sprang free and I reached for him, kneeling on the hard floor. I wasn't concerned about what the scratchy carpet would do to my knees; I just wanted to taste him.

I slid my mouth over the tip of his cock, smiling

as he threaded his fingers into my hair and tugged gently. I had to give it to my man, he let me enjoy him for several minutes before he pulled away.

"I'm not fin—" I never got the rest of my complaint out, as Reese gently laid me on the floor and thrust into me. All my breath left my body with an, "Ahhh."

His mouth claimed mine as he continued to surge into me, his hand cupping my breast before sliding down to finger my clit. I cried out as my orgasm hit, but didn't have time to enjoy it, as I was flipped onto my stomach. "Hips up, cheek to the floor, Lex."

My heart raced as I did as he directed. He lifted my hips higher and slid into me from behind and I lost my breath. Ohmigod, I'd forgotten how good this felt.

"Shhh, baby. Make it last."

"I... Reese," I hissed. He slapped my butt and I nearly came.

"Alexa," he warned in a whisper. "Don't come or you won't get more."

"Don't you dare stop," I snapped.

He chuckled, sliding partially out and then back in. "Control yourself."

I let out a frustrated groan and Reese gave me another three quick smacks on my bottom making me come so hard I lost my breath for a few seconds.

"Fuck me, baby," he breathed out, sinking deeper. "Your pussy's perfect."

I closed my eyes and nodded as Reese continued to move slowly, his hands settling on my hips, and slamming deeper and deeper, building another orgasm. He shifted slightly, sliding his hand to my belly. "Spread baby."

I spread and he lifted me, keeping his cock firmly

inside of me, so I was straddling him backwards. I dropped my head back, onto his shoulder and sighed.

"You okay?"

"Definitely. Yes," I panted.

With his left arm anchoring me against him, he rolled a nipple between his fingers while his right hand slid between my legs. I rose slightly, then lowered, slowing down when I feared another orgasm would hit. I wanted this one to last.

"That's right, baby," he whispered, and I raised up again, mewling as I slid back down. "Fuck," he rasped, and his finger found home.

He tapped my clit, then gently slapped at my pussy and the sting broke any control I had. I called out his name as I came and he pushed me back down and slammed into me, over and over, until he let out a satisfied groan, whispered, "Missed you, Freckles," and rolled us gently onto our sides in spoon fashion.

I wanted more, so I reached between my legs as I rocked my hips, dropping my head back against him.

"Greedy pussy," he whispered, replacing my hand with his, his finger going straight to my clit and bringing me to yet another perfect orgasm.

I sighed and rolled to face him. "If you ever make me miss this again, I will hunt you down and kill you."

He smiled, kissing my nose. "Not lettin' you go this time, baby."

"Correct answer."

"We'll need to figure something out, though. I'd like to fuck you in a bed going forward. No more of this office floor bullshit."

I chuckled. "I'll take you anywhere and any way I can."

"Appreciate that, baby, but you need somewhere soft to come. I'll make that happen, I promise."

I kissed him gently and stroked his cheek. "I've missed you."

"Same," he breathed out. "More than you can imagine."

"I highly doubt that."

He playfully smacked my bottom. "You don't think so?"

"The dumpee always has it worse."

"Technically, *you* dumped me," he countered.

"I did *not.*"

"At the risk of inciting your anger, baby, you absolutely dumped me. I just wanted to put some distance between us to keep you safe. You were the one who ended it."

"You gave me no choice," I hissed.

He sighed. "I don't want to fight, Lex."

"Then stop pissing me off," I snapped, and rose to my feet, dragging my habit back over my head.

"Fuckin' boner killer," Reese complained.

I glared at him. "I'll remember that for the future."

He rolled his eyes as he donned his clothes again and pulled me close. "Like I said, I don't want to fight."

I locked my body tight and shrugged. "Too late."

He lifted my chin. "I love you. I'm sorry you felt like the only choice you had was to end things. I hated that part, but I plan to make it up to you."

I relaxed slightly and studied him. "I did not dump you."

"Okay, Lex, we'll go with that."

"Reese—"

"Baby, I'm agreeing with you. Take yes for an answer."

I wrinkled my nose. "I just want you to admit I'm right."

"Four orgasms weren't enough?"

"Exactly what do orgasms have to do with you being wrong?" I challenged.

"I was hoping they'd make you forget we'd even been apart, ergo, no right or wrong concessions needed."

I bit back a smile. "The problem with four orgasms, sugar bear, is that they drive home exactly how much I've missed you. *Ergo*, you should admit you were wrong."

He dropped to his knees and pulled me against him, his face in my belly. "Oh, baby, please forgive me," he cried in a really bad southern accent. "I have been remiss in my duties to serve you."

I snorted weaving my hands in his hair. "Stand up, goofball."

"Not until you forgive me, Miss Alexa. I can't live without your favor and forgiveness."

"I forgive you, weirdo."

He grinned, standing again and kissing me deeply. "Thank you."

"Can we finish eating now?"

"Definitely."

We sat back down at the makeshift table and finished our now cold dinner. I didn't care. It was still delicious…as was my man.

I set my fork down and bit my lip. "Can I ask a favor?"

"Yeah."

"I really need to see Paisley," I said. "It's been forever. We have burner phones, but I really need to see her."

"There's a reason you can't see her, Lex."

"I know, but you've figured out how to get in. Can you do that for her?"

He sighed.

"*Please*, honey," I begged. "I miss her."

"I'll see what I can do."

I jumped up and leaned over to kiss him. "Thank you."

"Haven't done anything yet, Lex."

"But you will. I have faith."

He chuckled. "Finish your dinner."

"Yes, sir." I gave him a mock salute and finished my dinner.

Alexa

FOR THE NEXT week, I saw Reese every evening for dinner. He'd also brought me another burner phone so that I could call him if I needed to. We had our private time in the office just outside the chapel, and I relished it, even if I was forced to make love to him on a hard floor. I didn't mind. I just wanted to be with him.

The Saturday after our reunion, however, was a little different. I had been given permission to leave the Abbey for an overnight with him. I'm not sure if the Reverend Mother knew it was an overnight with Reese, or how much she knew about the whole affair in general, but I didn't care. It was an overnight. With my man. I almost peed with excitement.

I didn't have a whole lot in the way of street

clothes…I hadn't been able to take anything with me, so I was stuck with what I had been wearing when I came to my new home, and what I'd been able to procure from the donations pile. One pair of jeans, one pair of yoga pants, a couple of T-shirts and underwear, and a coat. Bare bones, considering I used to love to shop and had required two closets for all of my crap. I suppose I probably still loved to shop…I just hadn't done it in a while.

I did have some makeup and hair products, so I took special care with those…I shouldn't have, however. As soon as Reese arrived, he shoved a brunette wig and baseball hat toward me. "Disguise."

"But…but I look really good," I complained. "This will ruin it."

He chuckled. "Baby, you always look good. And you can fix your hair at my place."

I wrinkled my nose. "Fine, but I'm doing this under protest."

"Noted."

He helped me with the wig, which made me itch almost immediately, then he set the baseball cap on my head and took my hand. "You look gorgeous. Weird, but still gorgeous."

"Why weird?"

"Because my woman's blonde. I like blonde. You're just not a brunette. How will I find you in a crowd?"

I rolled my eyes. "You're not going to leave my side, so you won't *have* to find me in a crowd."

He grinned, leaning down to kiss me gently. "Good answer."

I squeezed his hand and we headed down into the tunnels. I shivered. They gave me the creeps.

"You scared?"

"You know how I feel about dark, creepy places."

He wrapped his arm around me. "I've got you."

I felt for the holster he usually kept on his waist and relaxed. "Okay, you're packin', I'm good."

He chuckled quietly. "The things your mouth does with words, baby…"

"I'll show you what my mouth does with other things, sugar bear, as soon as you get me the hell out of this place."

He kissed my temple and led me through the tunnels and several locked gates, then we exited out of a storm drain and into a wooded area. Of course, Reese made me wait before I was allowed *out* of the storm drain, so he could check the area.

"You're not expecting me to walk through the forest, are you?"

He chuckled, but didn't answer my question.

"Sugar bear," I said as saccharinely as I could. He didn't answer. "Um, sweetie pie?"

He grinned and shook his head.

"Ohmigod, you *do* expect me to walk through the forest."

"Lex." He stopped walking and faced me. "I know you. I know your aversion to walking. How about you just relax for a bit, yeah?"

"I'd relax more if you gave me a play-by-play of what we were doing."

He dropped his head back and stared at the trees. "Patience is a virtue. Patience is a virtue," he chanted.

I smacked his chest and he laughed, dropping his head down again to kiss me.

"Reese," I hissed, breaking the kiss. "How far do we have to walk?"

"Not far."

"Less than a mile?"

"Less than a half a mile," he said.

"Oh, okay. That's fine."

"Is it, m'lady?"

"Bite me, sugar bear."

He kissed me again and things got heated enough that we had to break apart…leaving me panting to catch my breath.

"Can't wait to get you into my bed."

"So you can bite me?" I asked, hopefully.

"So I can keep you naked for an entire night." He cocked his head. "Since when do you like biting?"

I saw his face redden a little and I shook my head. "I *don't* know if I like being bitten, I just figured since it's you, and I love being spanked, we could try it."

"Fuck me, Lex. We're tryin' to make a break for it and you get all sexy right now?"

"Sorry not sorry." I bit my lip and smiled. "But, seriously…the biting."

He took a second to adjust himself and then focused on me again. "Biting *might* be on the table, depending on how you handle walking through the forest."

"That's blackmail."

"No doubt," he agreed. "But it's really up to you, baby. Do you want to be spanked or bitten?"

Hell, yes, I did. However, I shrugged and said, "Whatever."

"My bike's just up here."

"We're taking your bike?"

"Yep."

I bit my lip. I'd missed his bike.

"Is there a problem?" he asked. I could tell his patience was wearing thin.

"Other than the fact I might come the second I'm on it?" I murmured. "No."

"Control yourself, baby. Your orgasms belong to me."

"Does the bike belong to you?"

He raised an eyebrow. "Baby, it's the same bike I've had since we were kids."

I shrugged. "Well, then if I come on the back of it, technically, it belongs to you."

"Fair enough."

I grinned in triumph. "I'm really glad to be back on your bike, honey."

"Me too, Lex." He stopped walking and turned to face me. "No one else has been on it since you."

I dropped my head to his chest. "I'm really happy to hear that."

He lifted my head and kissed me gently. "I love you, baby."

"Love you too."

He kissed me again and we continued to where he'd left his bike. I was almost as excited to get on the back of his Harley as I was to spend the night with him…almost. I loved riding with him. It was my second favorite thing to do.

Reese handed me a full-face helmet and I had to figure out how to get it over my wig. Luckily, he allowed me to remove my hat, but he made sure the wig hung down my back. I suppose to make it look like a brunette was on the back of his bike.

Admittedly, after the last couple of years of hiding out, I was no longer surprised by any of the strange subterfuge methods people used to keep me safe.

I hugged Reese tight as we rode through the streets of Portland, driving up to a little one-story house and the garage door opened. Reese pulled into the garage and tapped my leg for me to get off the bike. I dismounted and he killed the engine and set the kickstand down. Once he closed the garage door, he pulled off his helmet and helped me with mine.

"This is your house?" I asked.

"Yeah, baby. Do you like it?"

I nodded. "From the outside it looks gorgeous. I didn't think you'd ever move so close to the city, though."

"Ryder bought a house up here, so a couple of us followed."

"Ahh, that makes sense." I grinned. "You and Ryder and your bromance."

He chuckled. "He's my brother, baby."

"I know. I get it."

He took my hand and kissed the palm gently. "Come in and I'll show you around."

"What about my bag?"

"I'll get it later."

I nodded and followed him into the house expecting to find a bachelor pad…it was not. It was adorable. "Reese, this place is so cute."

He raised an eyebrow. "Cute?"

"Okay, maybe not 'cute.' Manly, but still very showhome-esque." I chuckled. "I was expecting a messy bachelor pad."

He grinned, leaning down to kiss me quickly. "The plan has always been to flip this place, so I had to appeal to buyers."

"You did all this work?"

"With a little help from the guys, yeah," he said.

"Come see the view."

He led me onto the back deck that overlooked the river and I gasped. "Reese, it's incredible."

He wrapped his arm around my waist and pulled me close, kissing my temple. "Yeah."

"Do you *have* to flip it?"

"No, why?"

I smiled up at him. "I want to live here."

"Yeah?"

I nodded.

"You gonna marry me?"

"Probably not," I breathed out.

"What the fuck?"

I patted his chest. "You haven't asked."

He grinned. "I'll figure out how to fix that."

"That'd be good."

He gave me one more squeeze and then we headed back inside. "You can take the wig off, Lex."

"Oh, thank God." I ripped it off my head and dropped it onto the sofa.

"If you go outside, though, you need to put it back on."

I cocked my head. "Are you worried about drones?"

"And passing boats…and zoom lenses," he admitted.

"I'll be careful. I promise."

"Thanks, baby." He stroked my cheek. "I have a surprise for you."

I clapped my hands. "I love surprises."

"I know you do."

He took my hand and led me down a bright hallway and into what appeared to be the master bedroom. The king-sized bed sat against the back wall facing sliding glass doors that opened onto the deck we had just been standing on. There were shear curtains that were closed, but still let light in, then heavier drapes pulled open to maximize the sunshine.

Sitting on the bed were shopping bags. Macy's, Nordstrom Rack, Target, and Anthropologie. "What did you do?" I squeaked.

"Did a little shopping," he said.

"I can see that."

"I want you to try everything on and I'll return whatever you don't like."

I blinked up at him. "Are you kidding me?"

"I know you don't have a whole lot right now and that you can't go shopping yourself, so I asked Paisley to help me find some things you might like."

"You did?"

"I did," he confirmed. "She'll also be comin' over later. Blake's gonna figure out a way to get her here without notice."

I clapped my hands and hugged him. "Really?"

"Yeah, baby."

"Thank you!"

"You're welcome. Now try on the shit."

I laughed and rushed for the goodies.

In the end, there was only one pair of jeans I didn't like, mostly because they made my bubble butt look flat and that was not acceptable to Reese.

He'd bought me two new pairs of jeans, a pair of tennis shoes, a gorgeous strappy pair of sandals, a pair of flats, a pair of knee-high boots, and a pair of heels that complemented my brand new little black dress (that I *really* hoped I'd get to wear soon outside of his house). There were also three pairs of leggings, a couple of skirts, four of the cutest tops I'd ever seen (Paisley's influence, obviously), six T-shirts, and underwear that would last a while. Both sexy and practical. The plan was to leave most of it at Reese's, but I couldn't resist shoving a few things into my backpack to take back with me to the abbey.

"Did you leave anything in the stores?" I asked, wrapping my arms around his waist.

"Not much, no." He kissed my head. "Are you happy?"

I met his eyes. "Honey, everything's perfect. This is all so unbelievably generous. Thank you."

"I got just as much out of this, you know?"

"You hate shopping, so how does that work, exactly?"

He smiled. "I got to watch you dress and undress over and over."

I flattened my palm over his growing erection and licked my lips. "Wanna return the favor?"

He picked me up and covered my mouth with his, carrying me to the bed. I guess I had my answer. Dropping me gently onto the mattress, he yanked off his shirt and stretched over me, pushing my T-shirt up over my head, freeing my mouth and nose, but using the fabric as a blindfold.

"No moving," he ordered, and I swallowed as I nodded. I felt pressure on my clit over the lace of my panties, then the sensation of the fabric being slid down my thighs almost broke me, and I had to force myself to breathe.

"Reese," I rasped.

"Shh, Freckles."

I squeezed my eyes shut behind the blindfold, doing my best to stop myself from letting out a frustrated growl. He pushed my knees apart and my legs shook as he covered my core with his mouth, sucking my clit gently as I arched up to get closer.

"You're moving, Alexa," he admonished.

I huffed, but set my butt back down on the mattress.

"Good girl," he said, and went back to his task.

He slid one finger inside of me, then two as he continued his assault on my clit. I panted out, "Oh, God, baby, I'm—"

"Don't come," he ordered.

I lost his fingers and let out a hiss of frustration. "Reese."

My hips were lifted slightly and then Reese filled me and I arched up to get more. I tried to slide my fingers into his hair, but he pushed my arms over my head, keeping the shirt firmly over my eyes. I whimpered with need, but he rolled a nipple before sucking on it gently and I sighed with pleasure.

"I want to touch you."

His hand slid between our bodies and he fingered my clit. "In a minute."

"*Now*," I breathed out.

The T-shirt slipped off my eyes and he grinned down at me. "Eager beaver."

"Damn straight my beaver's eager." I leaned up to kiss him. "Get this off of me." The shirt had now made it difficult for me to move my arms.

He pushed the shirt off my body and chucked it in the corner of the room as he kissed me deeply. His hand went back between our bodies and I knew I wouldn't be able to hold back for long. "Reese."

"Come, baby."

I did. He thrust into me a few more times and then

I felt his cock pulse inside of me and I held him tight as he kissed me again. He broke the connection and stared down at me, stroking my cheek. "I love you, Lex."

"I love you too, honey."

"Missed this."

I smiled up at him. "Me too."

"Can't let you go back."

"Can you make that happen?"

He sighed, dropping his forehead to mine. "I don't know."

Sliding out of me, he flopped onto his back and pulled me on top of him.

"I don't know how it would work," I admitted. "The trial isn't for months. I can't really see myself being out of the security of the abbey."

"I know." He held me tighter. "Me neither. Don't like it, though."

"Me neither," I mimicked.

He smiled. "You ruin me, baby."

"Back atya, sugar bear." I ran my finger down his chest. "Can we do this on a regular basis?"

"As often as we can, absolutely."

"I wish I could give my testimony over video now. I feel like I got you back and I don't want to have to wait to start our lives."

"I'm more concerned about another postponement."

"Ohmigod." I sat up with a gasp. "I hadn't even thought about that, which is dumb since I'm an attorney. There have already been three."

He dragged his hands down his face. "I know."

"Will they do it again, do you think?"

"No clue."

"Well, can we make a plan if they do postpone it?"

He leaned up on his forearms. "What kind of plan?"

"A plan for us," I said. "One that involves us being together every day. Not sneaking out of storm drains for X-rated interludes."

He grinned and tugged me back on top of him. "Yes."

"Promise?"

He rolled me onto my back and kissed my neck. "Even though I love X-rated interludes, I'd much rather be with you every day. So, yes, I promise."

"Correct answer."

I giggled when my stomach growled…loudly…and Reese sat up. "My woman's apparently hungry."

"Or I have gas," I countered.

"Have you suddenly developed irritable bowel syndrome?"

"I might if you don't feed me."

He dropped his head back and laughed before pulling me off the bed. "Come on, baby. Leave your clothes off."

"When is Paisley getting here?"

"Not for another two hours," he said.

"Mmm, naked cooking. I'm in…unless you plan to fry stuff."

"I will keep the hot oil down to a minimum," Reese promised.

"I appreciate that, sugar bear."

He kissed my neck. "No way in hell I'm marring this body."

I giggled. "Ulterior motives. Got it."

He pulled me close and leaned down to kiss me

gently. “Love you.”

“So you’ve said.”

He raised an eyebrow. “Am I being too romantical for you, Lex?”

“It’s been a long time, honey. You need to let me get used to your total adoration for me again.” I smiled. I was the least romantic person on the planet, something Reese used to tease me about mercilessly. “I’ve had to contend with only Paisley for years.”

He chuckled. “The only two women I know who hate romance more than most men.”

“So very, very true.”

“Come on, let me do the most romantic thing in the world and feed you.”

I stood on my tiptoes and kissed him. “Sounds good.”

Reese and I headed to the kitchen and managed to eat part of our food before he fucked me up against the kitchen counter then took me back to bed.

After several more orgasms, I showered and dressed in one of my new pairs of jeans and a soft T-shirt. Paisley arrived about twenty minutes later and I was introduced to Blake.

Blake was about six feet tall and held himself like a much bigger man. He had long silvery black hair he wore in a man-bun and he reminded me a lot of Anson Mount, complete with full beard and smirky smile. Every inch of skin visible was tattooed, including his neck, which was so very biker. I remember Reese mentioning he was fifteen years older than him, so he must be in his forties now, although, he looked much younger.

Alexa

A WEEK LATER, I was fully over being stuck in the abbey. I had only been able to see Reese twice since our overnight and it was killing me.

I was in the chapel, alone, placing hymnals in pews when Sadie walked in and headed toward me. "Hello, Sister Maria, how are you?"

"I'm well, Sadie. Thank you."

"I was wondering if you would like to join me and Ryder for dinner this evening."

My heart raced knowing that meant Reese time. "I would like that very much."

"Excellent. I'll pick you up around five." She wrinkled her nose as she lowered her voice. "You'll need to wear the wig with your veil and habit."

I sighed. "Okay, Sadie. I understand."

"Great. We'll see you tonight." She pulled me in for an awkward hug. "I'm so glad you're coming."

"Me too."

She gave me one more smile then left me standing next to the third pew from the back.

Finally.

I desperately needed to see my man.

* * *

Reese

I paced Ryder's living room waiting for Alexa to arrive. She was late and I was growing increasingly frustrated. Sadie had left over an hour ago and should have been back by now, but here I was still pacing the room. I should have collected her.

Ryder clapped me on the back and handed me a beer. "She'll be here, brother."

I took the bottle and sighed. "What's takin' so fuckin' long?"

Ryder chuckled. "You know Sadie drives like an old lady. She's bein' careful, but she got to the church and left about twenty minutes ago. She'll be—"

Before he could finish his pep talk, I caught motion on the cameras. Sadie's BMW started its ascent up the long driveway. I set my beer on the coffee table, pulled the drapes to the picture window closed, and waited inside the front door. Sadie walked in first, followed by Alexa who didn't have a second to greet Ryder because I grabbed her, tugging her veil and black wig from her head and kissing her deeply.

Alexa responded immediately, giggling against my mouth. "Hey."

"Hey. Missed you."

"Missed you too, honey."

"Please tell me you're wearin' somethin' else under that thing."

She raised an eyebrow. "This *thing* needs to be shown more respect."

I rolled my eyes. "It would be great, baby, if you wouldn't mind," I said carefully, "if you would so kindly take off your habit so I can make-out with you and not feel like I'm goin' to hell."

Sadie giggled behind us and the sound brought me back to the present. "Shit."

Alexa grinned and patted my face gently. "Kinda forgot she was there, huh?"

I sighed and forced a smile. "Little bit."

"Unzip me," Lex ordered, and turned her back.

I did as I was instructed and was rewarded with Alexa in jeans and a low-cut sweater that slid off one milky shoulder (which I leaned down and kissed gently). "Thanks, baby."

"My pleasure, sugar bear." She faced me with a smile and then picked up her discarded habit and veil, folding them neatly and setting them on the bench by the front door.

I caught Sadie grinning behind her hand, and I raised an eyebrow in challenge. She shook her head and could no longer hide her mirth. Waving her hand between me and Lex, she said, "I really like this, Reese."

I grinned. "Me too, Sadie."

After greeting Ryder, Alexa made her way back to me and wrapped her arms around my waist. I pulled her close and kissed her head before walking her (still attached to me) into the kitchen.

"Can I get you a glass of wine or a beer, Lex?" Sadie asked.

"Wine, please."

Sadie poured her a glass and tried to hand it to her, but I wouldn't release her to retrieve it. Alexa giggled. "I need to get closer to reach the sweet nectar, baby…"

Instead of letting her go, I shuffled us both closer to the kitchen island.

"You're ridiculous Reese," Alexa complained but didn't loosen her grip on my waist.

I kissed her temple in response.

"Was he like this back in the day?" Sadie asked Ryder.

Ryder wrapped his arms around her waist from behind her. "Yeah, baby, he was."

Sadie's eyes widened. "Wow," she whispered.

Alexa chuckled. "It was out of control back then, too."

"Hey now," I admonished.

"You can growl at me all day long, Mr. Alden," Alexa said as she craned her neck to look up at me. "But it doesn't make it any less true."

I smiled down at her and kissed her nose. "Gonna grab my beer. Don't move."

"Exactly where would I go?"

I didn't answer her rhetorical question as I headed to the living room and grabbed the beer I'd earlier discarded. When I walked back to the kitchen, Alexa was at the stove helping with dinner.

"You moved," I accused, and she glanced over her shoulder with a laugh.

"Technically, I didn't move, honey. I *stepped* to the stove."

"Are you arguing semantics?"

"Damn skippy I am," she retorted.

I grinned and kissed the nape of her neck, whispering, "Wish I could get you naked."

"I heard that," Sadie said.

I laughed. "I don't care."

Alexa reached around me and smacked my ass. "Behave."

"No promises."

She faced me and kissed my neck. "How about you and Ryder go bond and I'll help Sadie with dinner?"

"I spend a lot of time with Ryder," I complained. "I'm good right here."

"But if you're here, I can't talk about *you*."

"Sure you can." I took a swig of my beer.

"I'm not going anywhere, honey." Alexa squeezed my hand. "Go relax."

I studied her and then shook my head, leaning down to kiss her. "Fifteen minutes."

"Twenty."

"Fourteen."

"You can't give me *less* time," she argued.

I sighed dramatically. "Sixteen, then."

She giggled. "Fine…sixteen."

I stared at her a little longer, then left the kitchen.

* * *

Alexa

"Oh, my word," Sadie whispered. "I have never seen him like that."

I chuckled. "He's a little over the top, huh?"

"It's adorable," she said. "Can you believe he

scared the bejesus out of me when I met him?"

I washed tomatoes and started to slice them on the cutting board. "He did?"

"It's not hyperbole when I say Reese was angry. I never saw him smile."

"He's had a tough life."

"Ryder alluded to that too, and you certainly don't have to share, but I'm really glad that you're back in it." She smiled gently. "He's happy, Lex."

"Me too." I sighed. "Although, I kind of wish I'd made him suffer a little longer."

"Really?"

I nodded. "Yes. But the problem was, I missed him like crazy and I couldn't fake *not* missing him. I *did* try, but I have never been a particularly good liar."

"Me neither," Sadie admitted.

"And especially to him. He can read me like a book."

Sadie dumped lettuce into a large bowl. "Ryder's the same way with me. It's a little annoying."

I grinned. "Right?"

"Well, I'm glad you're back. I adore Reese and he deserves to be happy."

"He really does, Sadie," I breathed out. "He's the best person I've ever known."

"He's a really good guy."

I nodded. "Even when his dad forced him to do shit for the Spiders, he refused to do anything illegal. It's the reason he did what he did. He didn't want to be a prospect and the pressure was getting intense." I gasped. "God, I just realized what a bitch I've been."

"I highly doubt that," Sadie countered.

"I should have been more patient," I admitted. "I was so wrapped up in my hurt feelings that I wasn't willing to see his point of view. I was so mean to him, Sadie."

She just smiled, but didn't respond.

"Will you excuse me for a minute?"

Sadie nodded and I went to find Reese. He was on the deck with Ryder, so I pushed open the slider and rushed to him, wrapping my arms around his waist from behind. "I'm sorry."

"Hey," he said, turning to face me. "What's wrong?"

"I'm really sorry."

"About what?"

"You really need to get in the house, Lex," Ryder warned.

Reese lifted me so my feet dangled by his shins and I wrapped my arms around his neck as he carried me back into the house and down the hall.

Stepping into a guest bedroom, Reese pulled me close and lifted my chin. I was determined not to cry, but I could feel the burn behind my nose.

"Talk to me."

I bit my lip. "I should have listened to you."

"When?" he asked.

I could no longer hold back the flood and burst into ugly, sobby tears. "Back when you tried to put some distance between us. I shouldn't have broken things off. We could have made it work. I should have trusted you." He wiped my cheeks as I continued to cry. "I'm so sorry, Reese. I was such a bitch."

"You weren't a bitch, baby."

I nodded. "I was. I totally was."

He chuckled leaning down to kiss my wet cheeks. "Freckles, you were hurt and scared. I never blamed you."

"Well, you should have."

"Can't blame the only woman I've ever loved. Especially since you didn't do anything wrong. It wasn't your choice to be born into a crime family."

"It wasn't your choice either."

"I know, baby, but if hurting you was the end result of getting out, it wasn't worth it."

I bobbed my head up and down. "I get that now. I would have done the same thing."

"I know you would."

"And you would have been gracious and way nicer to me."

"You think so, huh?"

I nodded. "I totally do."

"Well, we can't change the past, so let's not dwell there, okay?"

"I'm still sorry."

"I appreciate that, honey…even though you don't need to be."

I licked my lips then kissed him and he lifted me high enough so I could wrap my legs around his waist. Our kiss turned desperate and he broke the connection with a frustrated groan. "Fuck, baby."

"Yes, please."

"Can't do this in Sadie and Ryder's house."

"I get it." I kissed him one more time. "I really missed you, though. I still kind of miss you."

"Me too, Lex. I'll fix it."

I smiled and stroked his cheek. "Your fix-it list is getting longer by the day."

"I'm aware."

I smiled and slid down his body, back to my feet. "I trust you."

"Good." He raised my chin and met my eyes.

"You okay?"

"Yeah, honey, I'm good."

"Dinner ready?"

I gasped. "Crap. I kind of abandoned Sadie."

"It's okay. Take a minute. We'll head out when you're calmer."

"I'm calm, sugar bear." I linked my fingers with his. "I'm good."

He kissed me again and we headed back out to the kitchen. God bless Sadie, she didn't ask any questions…just let us have our moment without intrusion.

Under the close and watchful eye of my man, I helped Sadie with the rest of dinner. Even Reese and Ryder feigned assistance, and carried everything to the table. Once we sat down to eat, Reese grabbed my hand under the table briefly, leaning over to kiss my cheek and whispering, "I love you."

"Love you, too," I said.

* * *

Reese dropped me back at the abbey a little after midnight. It had been a near perfect night, but I was exhausted and fell into bed with a grateful sigh. It didn't take long to fall asleep, but I was awoken by the buzz of my burner phone about two hours later.

I sat up with a start, realizing it wasn't Reese calling, but Paisley. Paisley *never* called, so it must be important. I kicked off the covers and rose to my feet. "Paisley? You okay?"

A deep voiced chuckle came over the line. "Hello, beautiful Alexa."

"Who is this?" My stomach churned. "Where's Paisley?"

Paisley screamed, "*Lex, don't list—*"

I heard a slap and the man yelled, "*Zatknis*!" (Shut up!)

"Paisley!" I hissed.

"You're to do everything I tell you," he demanded.

"Or what?" I snapped.

"We'll kill her, Alexa. Don't doubt it."

I closed my eyes and took a deep breath. "What do you want?"

"We want you to retract your statement. Refuse to testify."

"And if I don't?"

"Your friend will die," he said. "You have until noon to contact the FBI, and tell them you no longer wish to testify. If you do not, or you involve the authorities, I will send you pieces of your friend in the mail for a year."

The line went dead.

I needed Reese. I grabbed my other phone and dialed his number. He didn't answer right away, which only caused my anxiety to rise. I waited a few seconds and tried again. This time he answered. "You miss me?" he asked.

"Reese," I rasped.

"Baby, what's wrong?"

"Paisley. The Russians have her. I just got a phone call."

"What?"

I paced my room. "The call history says number unknown and I have no idea who has her or where she is."

"Okay, baby. It's okay. Tell me everything he said."

I filled him in on the conversation, panicking more and more as I relayed it.

"Lex."

"They have her, Reese. They're going to kill her!"

"Lex."

"She's my best friend, you have—"

"Alexa!" he snapped.

"What?"

"We're gonna find her. But you need to promise me something."

"*Okay*," I said suspiciously.

"You have to stay put."

"I—"

"Lex," he said again. "Do *not* leave the abbey under any circumstance."

I sighed. "Where would I go?"

"Alexa."

"Fine, I won't leave the abbey," I promised. "But you have to keep me updated."

"I will, baby."

"Please find her, Reese," I whispered.

"I'm gonna do that. Promise."

He hung up and I squeezed my eyes shut and sat down on my bed.

Reese

I HUNG UP with Alexa and immediately dialed Hatch.

"It's two a.m., you better have a damn good reason why you're wakin' me," he growled.

I filled him in on everything Lex had told me.

"This is going to be tough," Hatch said. "Burner phones can't easily be traced, if at all, but I'll put Booker on it."

"I had trackers put in each of the phones," I said. "Unless those scumbags physically crack Paisley's phone open, they'll never know it's there, and will assume the phones are untraceable."

"Shit, man, the FBI's got you thinking like a cop now. What can I do to help?"

"Meet me at the compound," I said. "I'll call Ryder and have him bring some extra fire power."

"What exactly are we walking into?"

"No clue," I admitted. "But I want to be prepared for anything. This has to be kept between the three of us for now. Don't let anyone see you leave your place and don't ride your bike."

"Gotta read the prez in, brother."

"Only Crow, then," I snapped.

"Understood," Hatch replied.

"We're going to get Paisley back by any means necessary, and we have to do it without the FBI or the local police involved. If they see us or the cops coming, they'll kill her."

"I get it, man. I'll see you in a bit," Hatch said.

I hung up and got dressed. I couldn't waste any time. I grabbed my truck keys and headed out the door. My mind was foggy due to the late hour, but I needed to think of a plan, and fast. The tracker app on my phone showed me Paisley was being held in an industrial area of Gresham, right in the heart of Spiders territory, an area I was all too familiar with.

What the fuck is going on here?

The Russian Mob and the Gresham Spiders together in the same area? There was no way this could be a coincidence, but I had no idea what it all meant. I pulled into the Dog's compound and called Alexa to give her a quick update before going inside.

"Did you find her?" she asked, her voice desperate.

"I have a pretty good idea where she is."

"What can I do?"

"Just stay put. I'm gonna get her and then I'll call you. If you don't hear from me, don't freak out, okay?"

She sighed. "I trust you. But be careful."

"I will, baby. Talk to you soon."

I hung up and walked into the building. Hatch, Ryder, and Booker met me in the back conference room. I was surprised to see Hawk and a young kid I didn't recognize there as well.

"You weren't keepin' me out of this," Hawk growled.

I smiled. "I appreciate the support, brother."

He nodded.

"This is Devon," Hatch explained. "My nephew and prospect for the club. He was at our place when you called, so I figured he could get some hands-on experience."

"Right," I said.

"What's the plan?" Ryder asked the moment I walked through the door.

"First, we have to zero in on exactly where Paisley is." I handed my phone to Booker. "I need you to use the tracking app, and let me know exactly where she's being held. The general coordinates are not enough. I need you to tell me the exact address, down to the room she's in if possible. The Spiders have several buildings in that vicinity, so it could be any of them."

"I'm on it."

"Ryder, I need you to load up the van. We need shotguns, flash grenades, tear gas and masks for all of us. I have one more phone call to make. Wheels up in twenty."

I walked into the hallway and dialed a number I hadn't called in a while.

"Yeah?" the gruff voice answered.

"Frogger, it's Reese."

Frogger's father was also an officer in the Gresham Spiders and we'd been recruits together. I got out and he didn't. Nonetheless, he was a good guy and always had my back. I didn't blame Frogger for staying in, as his father would have likely put him in the hospital, or worse, if he didn't follow him into the family business. Still, I knew his loyalty to the club only ran so deep and I was betting that his loyalty to me was deeper. In fact, I was betting Paisley's life on it.

"Reese? Is that really you? Fuck man, what time is it?"

"Can I still trust you?" I asked.

"What? Of course you can, man, what the fuck's going on?"

"I mean it, Erik, can I trust you?"

He obviously knew I meant business and the sleep left his voice immediately. "What do you need?"

"I need information. I need to know if the Spiders are working with the Russian mob."

"Shit man, what the fuck are you involved with?"

"Are they working together?" I snapped.

"Yeah, man, I think so. I'm not sure, but there have been a lot of dudes around with Russian accents. I just figured they were here for the girls, but I guess they could be mob guys."

"What girls?" I asked.

"The club has been dealing in girls more and more over the past few years. Hookers, porn, web cams, whatever," he explained. "These Russian guys always seem to have a hand in what's going down when girls are involved, but no one has said shit to us about who they are."

"What else?"

"What do you mean, what else?" he grumbled. "I dunno, man. I don't know who these chicks are or where they came from any more than the last batch, or the group that went missing."

"Missing?"

"Yeah, man. A bunch of girls escaped a while back and Prez's been on the warpath to find them ever since."

Rusty Kross was the Spiders' ruthless president and the main reason for the abbey's high rate of occupancy. The other members of the "Nuns on the Run" program were in hiding from the Russians. Obviously, the Spiders' FBI mole had dug deeper than we thought and the girls were in more danger than ever. I was pretty sure they still didn't know about the abbey, but would make sure we had more muscle there than just "Father Michael."

"Do you know anything about a girl being held by the old clubhouse?"

"No, man, but like I said, they leave us out of that side of the business. We run dope and guns, and they take care of the girls along with Putin's friends."

I rubbed my forehead and paced the hallway. "If someone was being guarded at the old clubhouse, how many members, do you think, would be there?"

"These days? Shit, man, with Rusty's paranoia…if something went down, he'd be ready for war."

"That's what I thought."

"You're not thinking of doing something stupid are you?" he challenged. "You almost got killed getting out, and the only reason you're still alive is because your pops is dead. No one's heard a peep from you, and your low profile has kept you off Rusty's shit list. Well, until now. But if you come around and start shit, Rusty'll publicly gut you just to prove a point."

"I don't doubt that for one second. Thanks, brother. Keep your head down."

I hung up and headed back inside.

* * *

Alexa

Reese had kept his promise and called me to update me, but I still felt sick to my stomach. We'd been so careful! Paisley was protected, both at home and work, so who the hell got to her and how? I hated not having answers to these questions, but for now I was stuck trusting my man.

Which I did.

In theory.

I was never very good at sitting still and waiting for anything. Instant gratification was my middle name, and right now sucked.

A quiet knock came at my door and I opened it to find Sadie.

"What are you doing here?" I asked.

"Ryder's orders. He wants me protected, so I'm here and Ollie's with Scottie," she said. "Feel like raiding the fridge with me?"

"I'd rather raid someone's liquor cabinet."

She giggled and whispered, "I know a place. C'mon, I'll buy you a drink."

"Lead the way, oh fallen one."

We tiptoed into the sanctuary and found the wine stowed behind the altar, which we opened with the corkscrew sitting next to it. We sat up against the wall and took turns sipping from the bottle. I was surprised by the vintage and surmised someone around here had a taste for something a bit finer than you'd expect in church.

"Do you know what's going on?" I asked.

"Only that Paisley's been taken, and Reese and Ryder are going to get her back," Sadie said.

"That's it?" I demanded.

"Yeah, Lex, that's it."

"Well, you're of no use to me, then."

She smiled. "Reese'll fill you in when they get her."

"If he doesn't get himself killed," I ground out.

Sadie gasped. "He's not going to die, Lex."

"Well, he better not…or I'll end him."

"Come on, Alexa, you're a pretend nun. Pretend to have a little faith. Reese knows what he's doing."

I bit back tears. "I know. I just want to see him, and I want to know Paisley's okay."

Sadie wrapped an arm around my shoulders. "You will before you know it."

I nodded. "I hope so. I just don't know if I'm strong enough for all of this."

Sadie raised her head and sighed. "And I don't know if I can do *this*, Lex."

"Do what?"

"Drink stolen wine underneath Jesus."

I looked up and forced back a laugh. We were sitting underneath the cross that displayed a very lifelike crucified Euro messiah. "Would it help if I told you it's really nice wine?"

"No, I think that makes it worse."

"Um…let's take this back to my room."

She nodded and we both rose to our feet.

"I certainly hope there aren't nuns in here drinking

the blood of the Lord," Father Michael growled as he walked through the door. "And I really hope there aren't nuns drinking a certain priest's 2007 Fontodi Flaccianello Sangiovese."

Sadie gasped, but I just chuckled. "No nuns here…no priests either."

He dropped his head back and laughed. "You got me there."

Father Michael wasn't really a priest. Michael wasn't even his real name. I didn't know what his real name was, but it wasn't Michael. He was an under-cover agent working for the FBI…for what purpose, I wasn't sure, but Summer and I (along with Annie and Taylor, the other two material witnesses) had been "read-in" so to speak when we were brought here. Should we have issues, he was our go-between.

"Anything I can do for you ladies, I mean "sis-ters," tonight?"

"Do you have another bottle hidden somewhere?" I asked.

"There's a reason I only kept one back there," he said.

"So, people like me can only steal one at a time?" I challenged.

"Something like that. Thanks to you, I have to find a new hiding place."

"It wasn't a very good one anyway," I challenged. "We found it, didn't we? Plus, what if someone acci-dentally uses it on Sunday?"

"I figured I'd hide it in plain sight. Kind of like you good sisters."

Michael let us take the wine and we headed to the kitchen, grabbed glasses, then headed back to my room to wait out the night. I wanted to tell Michael everything about Paisley's abduction, but Sadie was right, I needed to trust Reese. Plus, the kidnappers had said not to contact law enforcement and I had already taken a big enough risk telling Reese.

Reese

WE PULLED UP to the non-descript industrial park just before three in the morning. I cut the van's engine and headlights and coasted silently to a stop about fifty yards shy of the location where Paisley was being held. This location was once used as the Spiders' base of operation. Several buildings, which mostly appeared abandoned, made up the compound. The Spiders still owned the property, and even though they had moved their clubhouse to a more secure location a while back, from my phone call with Frogger, I knew this place was a hotbed of activity of newcomers and Russian mob types.

"Okay, according to Booker, it looks like Paisley's phone is in that building to the south west," Hatch said, pointing to what had once been a machine shop.

"I'm going to go take a look around and try to see how many assholes they have inside. You guys stay here and I'll be right back." I grabbed one of the sawed-off shotguns Ryder brought, quietly got out of the van, and walked toward the machine shop. The cover of the morning's darkness concealed my movements, which was my only protection at this point. The one advantage we had was the element of surprise and we needed to keep it that way.

I was dead silent as I approached the building, which is more than I could say for whoever was now following me. I could hear faint footsteps behind me, and I quickened my pace, but not enough to tip off whoever was following me. As he closed the distance between us, I spun around on my heels and pointed the scatter gun toward my would-be attacker.

He stopped dead in his tracks before raising his hands and whispering, "Reese, it's me Frogger. Don't shoot me, man."

I lowered the gun…slightly. "Frogger, what the fuck are you doing here?"

"I figured there was no way you were just gonna call me in the middle of the night, ask a bunch of questions about club business and this place, without coming down here yourself."

I was happy to see Frogger hadn't changed one bit. He got his name when he was a recruit. He was a couple years older than me and was lookin' for somethin' to belong to, which made him a prime target for the Spiders. Brick had insisted I check out the process, even though I had no intention of patching in, but I had to play the game until I could figure a way out, so I did what I was told.

As a candidate, the first week is hell, and every week after that just gets harder. For the first three weeks, Erik and I were mostly stationed at a house that we dealt arms out of. It was right across the way from a twenty-four-hour liquor store, which was great news for a bunch of bikers. What wasn't great, was eight lanes of busy freeway that divided our house and that shitty liquor store. It became Erik's job to take the member's orders and run across the freeway to get to the store as fast as possible. The OGs said he was so good at it, he reminded them of the old video game Frogger, and that was that. Erik was Frogger.

"Thanks, but I don't need your help," I said.

"I'm not here to help you," he retorted. "I'm here to stop you from doing whatever the fuck it is you're doing."

"I appreciate it, but like I said—"

"Whatever stunt you're trying to pull off is gonna get you killed. I checked and there are two big-ass Russians in there, along with at least three club members. There may even be more, so marching in there alone is suicide."

"Who said I was alone?" I challenged. I wasn't sure if Frogger was being straight with me or setting me up, but figured he wouldn't move on me if he knew I had backup.

"You'd better get them the hell outta here too, then. I'm telling you, man, the club is brutal these days. Worse than before even."

I stood a little straighter. "Help me get in there."

"Are you fucking insane?" he snapped. "Didn't you listen to a word I just said?"

"Listen, there's a woman inside and I've gotta get her out. She's gonna die if I don't. Do you hear me?

An innocent woman is gonna die if we can't get to her. I can't call the cops and I can't do this alone. I've got guys with me, but in order for this to work, I need to get in that shop undetected."

"Why the fuck would I help you, Reese? Why would I risk my life in order to help you ambush my brothers?"

"Because they're not your brothers and you know it. You hate this club almost as much as I do, but you stayed in order to survive. I get it, but now you've gotta make a choice once again. Leave the club and join me, or know that you're helping to kill, torture, and rape countless women. You know I'm right or you wouldn't have showed up here, too."

Frogger stood silently for a few seconds, barely able to make eye contact.

"Who the fuck is this?" Hatch growled, still being careful to whisper. He and Ryder were now flanking Frogger, with their guns drawn.

"Frogger," Ryder said,

"It's okay guys, put your guns down, he's with me," I stared at Frogger and raised an eyebrow. *Right*?

"Goddammit," he finally said. "There's a side door that's always locked, but I have a key. It leads directly to the shipping and receiving area, which is now used as old bike storage. There shouldn't be anyone in that room, so you can slip in without anyone seeing you." He took the key off his ring and handed it to me.

"Thank you."

"Don't thank me," he said. "You're gonna get you and your friends killed. Once the guys in there spot you, they'll mow you all down."

"Don't you worry about us," I said. "You worry

about you."

"Come on man," he said with a weird chuckle. "You know I'm just the crazy sonofabitch for the job. Good luck, Reese."

"I don't need luck. I've got a pack of nuns on my side."

Frogger cocked his head.

I shook my head. "Long story, I'll explain later."

We went back to the van, collected what we needed, and silently headed toward the shop. Once outside our entry point, we took a moment to go over the plan. We'd only have one shot at this, and our timing had to be perfect. I unlocked and opened the side door and Hatch, Ryder, and I quietly slipped inside, while Frogger made his way to the front door.

Once inside, I heard activity and voices coming from several rooms. Before we could make our move, however, we needed to figure out exactly where Paisley was, and we needed to do it fast.

Just then, a knock at the front door sent the building's occupants into a frenzy of activity. I used this opportunity to crack open the door into the hallway, and from my viewpoint I could see a sliver into the front room.

"Who the fuck is that?" I heard one man ask. I could also hear several men with heavy Russian accents shouting to one another.

The front door was opened, and I could now clearly hear Frogger's voice. "Hey guys, Prez asked me to come by to see if you needed anything."

"Who is this and what the fuck is he doing here?" one of the Russian men asked.

"Relax, he's one of us," another man responded, before adding, "But I don't know what the fuck he's doing here either."

"I just told you, Tiny," Frogger said. "Rusty sent me to check up on you. You guys need me to do a beer run or anything?"

"A beer run? It's four in the fucking morning," Tiny replied, and pulled out his cell phone. "You shouldn't even be here. I'm calling Rusty to find out what the fuck is going on."

"Sure, no problem, you do that, and I'm just gonna use the head real quick," Frogger said and started down the hallway toward the back rooms.

"Hey, don't go down there," Tiny's booming voice protested, as his massive frame lumbered after him, but Frogger was five steps ahead. I heard him open several of the office doors, stopping after the third.

"Oh, excuse me!" Frogger exclaimed loudly.

I could hear the muffled sounds of a woman's voice, as if she was gagged or her mouth was taped shut.

"Oh, sorry man, I didn't realize you were entertaining company in here, I was just looking for the john," Frogger said, making sure he was loud enough for us to hear.

"I said, get the fuck out of there," Tiny shouted as he rushed Frogger.

"Masks on," I mouthed to Hatch and Ryder. This was the moment I had been waiting for. I knew where Paisley was, and our enemy was distracted. I cracked the door open a little more, pulled the pin on one flash grenade, and made sure the safety was off on my riot gun. We had our masks on and it was show time. I pulled the pin and rolled the flash grenade down the hall. As soon as it detonated, I swung the door open and fired a tear gas canister toward the front room. Hatch was right behind me and tackled Tiny in the hallway just as we pushed through.

At least he *tried* to tackle him. Hatch was no small man by any means, but this was kind of a Thor vs. Hulk kind of moment here. Hatch slammed into Tiny, who barely seemed to move. He punched Hatch in the gut, winding him instantly, and causing his mask to fog up. He loaded up his right hand for a skull crushing blow and I let loose both barrels of my sawed-off shotgun. It was impossible to miss his center mass, and he flew backward, having taken the full impact of the blast.

My stunned party looked at me, then to Tiny, and then back to me again.

"Fucker's lucky it was loaded with rock salt," I ground out, and pushed open the door holding Paisley.

"Yeah," Ryder agreed.

"Get Paisley!" I yelled to Ryder as I shot a second canister down the hall.

She was coughing violently as Ryder picked her up and carried her out into the hall. Her hands, feet and mouth were duct taped, and her eyes were bloodshot and streaming with tears.

"Let's get the fuck outta here!" Hatch yelled as he helped Frogger to his feet.

Frogger was doubled over, blinded by the gas and barely able to breathe. The four of us made it out of the side door we'd entered through, and began running toward the van. Ryder was still carrying Paisley, and Hatch was with Frogger a few steps behind me. I looked behind us and could see one of the Russians just outside the doorway we had fled through. He raised his gun toward our group and began firing. I turned around and fired my last canister toward the building, which connected with his skull just after he got off a final shot. He fell to the ground and lay motionless.

I began running again and caught up with the others at the van. We piled in, Ryder cranked the engine, and sped off into the blackness. My ears were ringing from the gunfire. Paisley looked okay from what I could see but was coughing furiously from the tear gas. Her eyes were swollen and the skin around her mouth was red from the duct tape.

Ryder had cut her bindings off and she was reaching for her eyes.

"Don't rub them, babe," I warned. "It'll make it worse."

"It burns so bad." She squinted at me, her legs bobbing up and down as though to distract herself.

"I know. I'm so sorry," I said. "We had no other way of getting you out of there. Frogger, can you get her bottled water? Frogger…Frogger!"

"Reese!"

I turned to see Hatch on the floor of the van, holding Frogger, who was passed out and bleeding profusely from the stomach. "He's been shot, Reese. That big Russian fucker got him before you took him out."

I opened a water bottle and handed it to Paisley who poured it over her eyes while I crawled to Frogger. "How bad is it, Hatch?"

Hatch pulled off his shirt and used it to soak up the blood while pressing on the wound. "It looks like he was shot through and through. I don't think he hit the spine, but he's bleeding pretty bad, man, we've gotta get him to a hospital."

"Keep pressure on it." I pulled out my phone and dialed Cameron.

"Reese?"

"Hey, man, I've got a situation."

"Is Lex okay?" he asked.

"Yeah, but Paisley was taken and in the middle of getting her back, one of our guys got shot. Don't want to take him into the hospital without cover…they'll ask questions."

"Why didn't you call me first?" he ground out.

"No cops."

He sighed. "I'm gonna have to make a call. I'm still not in town."

"Shit!"

"Give me a few."

He hung up and I pulled my shirt off, replacing Hatch's with mine.

Paisley groaned and Devon grabbed another bottled water, this time pouring it on her eyes for her. "Let me do it, babe," he demanded when she tried to help. "You're dumping more on the ground than your face."

My phone rang again a few minutes later and Hatch took over putting pressure on Frogger. It was Cam.

"Hey, man," I said.

"Hey. Head over to Legacy…Dallas Stone will meet you there. His brother's the ER doc on duty and Dallas's wife, Macey's on shift. She's an RN."

"Okay, thanks, man."

"What'd he say?" Hatch asked.

"Legacy…Dallas'll meet us there."

Hatch nodded. "Is Macey on?"

I nodded.

"Good, she's Pay's best friend. She'll keep this under wraps."

"That's what I'm hoping."

We headed off to the hospital, Ryder driving while Hatch and I took care of Frogger.

* * *

Alexa

About three hours later, my phone rang, and I answered immediately. "Did you find her?"

"Yeah, baby, we got her," Reese said. He sounded wrecked.

I burst into tears. "Is she okay?"

"You can see for yourself. We'll be there in five minutes."

"Are you coming through the tunnels?"

"Yeah."

I swallowed. "Okay, I'll meet you at the entrance."

"Okay. See you in a bit."

I hung up and left my room, heading for the tunnel entrance. Sadie followed.

"Is she okay?" she asked.

"I don't know," I admitted. "I think so."

It took a lot longer than five minutes, but Reese walked in with a battered and bruised Paisley and I pulled her in for a gentle hug. "Are you okay?"

"I'm fine, Lex," she said, but sounded pissed. Her face was puffy and red and she looked like she'd been through hell. "God damn it, my eyes are still burning."

"You need to rinse them more," Reese said.

"You think so, asshole?"

"What's going on?" I asked Reese.

"Oh, you want to know what's going on?" Paisley

hissed, and glared up at Reese before looking back at me. "I am now a nun."

I gasped. "What?"

"She's on the Russians' radar now," Reese explained. "So, she's here until she's not."

"Ohmigod, dickhead," Paisley snapped. "I have a *job*! I can't just disappear."

"Cameron Shane's gonna take care of that part."

"Why are you with him, Lex?" Paisley seethed.

I smiled. "Because I love him…even if he's a pain in the ass."

"Hey," Reese countered.

Paisley fished her phone out of her pocket. "I need to call—"

"No calls," Reese interrupted.

Paisley stomped her foot and then whimpered in pain.

"What happened?" I demanded.

"It's a sprain," Paisley said. "Courtesy of the Gresham Spiders and tear gas burns to my eyes, thanks to your 'man.'"

"Macey checked her out and there's no damage to her eyes," Reese explained. "She might need to continue to rinse her eyes for the next few hours, though."

"Thanks for man-splaining that to her and talking about me as though I'm not here," Paisley hissed.

"How about we get you off that leg and get you some water to flush your eyes?" I suggested. "Anything broken?"

"Nothing broken, just bruises. Doc sent home pain meds." Reese handed me a paper bag.

Paisley huffed. "Who's going to grab my stuff? Water my plants? Feed my cat?"

"You don't have a cat," I retorted.

"*Alexa,*" she hissed.

"Someone'll take care of your place, Paisley, but this is not up for discussion." Reese leaned down to kiss me quickly, before facing Sadie. "Sadie, you need to come with me. I'm takin' you back to your place."

"Um, okay," she said.

Reese leaned down and kissed me again. "I'll call you later, baby."

"But…" I started, but he and Sadie walked away and left me and Paisley standing in the hallway. I sighed and wrapped an arm around her waist. "Let's get you settled. You can bunk with me until we know everything that's going on."

We hobbled back to my room where I wrapped her ankle again and she filled me in on her horrific night.

"Are you in pain?" I asked.

"A little."

"When can you have pain meds?"

"Now, probably," she said.

I smiled and grabbed her a glass of water. "Here."

She took the water and downed a pill, then dropped her head back against the wall. "They don't know about you."

"What do you mean?"

"Reese thought they might have figured out your hiding place, but they haven't."

"He told you this?"

She looked at me and rolled her eyes. "I overheard him and his cronies discussing."

I chuckled. "Of course you did."

"He's pissing me off, Lex. I know he's your obsession and all, but I'm not a fan."

I smiled and sat beside her on the bed. "I get it,

Paisley, and I know the history you two have, but believe it or not, he's trying to protect you."

"I didn't ask for it."

"No, but *I* did, honey."

"Well, you're a dick," she snapped.

I giggled. "I've heard that on a few occasions."

She gave me a slight smile, probably because she was so swollen she couldn't smile wide. "Ow."

"Let's get some ice on those bruises, huh?"

She nodded and we headed to the kitchen.

Alexa

TWO MONTHS LATER, with the trial looming earlier than expected, I found myself edgy and downright miserable. Paisley had been released to go to work each day, but she was here in the evening, and under heavy guard anytime she left the abbey, so I didn't have my partner in crime during the day, and couldn't see Reese much either. No one in my wake was safe, not even the Reverend Mother, which was why I was currently sitting in my room sobbing because I'd been so nasty to her.

A knock at my door brought Sadie and I frowned. "When did you get here?"

"About twenty minutes ago," she said. "Tough day, huh?"

I dropped my face in my hands. "Ohmigod, I totally freaked out on your aunt. I don't even know why."

Sadie giggled. "Oh, honey, it's okay. She didn't take it personally."

"Maybe she should have. I'm horrible."

"Alexa, you're stressed. The trial date's been moved up and you're understandably freaked out."

"That's no excuse to snap at the Reverend Mother because she offered me a sandwich."

Sadie giggled. "Well, you were pretty adamant about the salami, granted. But it's okay. Seriously. I know my aunt. She gets it."

I faced her. "I really need Reese."

"I know, honey, but it's not safe."

"I need him!" I growled.

"Call him."

"I already did. It didn't help. I need him here."

She wrapped an arm around my shoulders and rubbed my arm. "I'm sorry, Lex."

I shrugged her off of me. "I don't want you to be sorry, Sadie. I want you to figure out how to get my man here...*now*."

My stomach roiled and I was forced to make a run for the bathroom. My thoughts swirled as I puked up everything I'd eaten that day...the most urgent one being, if Sadie didn't get Reese here tout de suite, I was gonna cut a bitch.

I washed my face and brushed my teeth, then headed back into my room. It was empty and I breathed a sigh of relief as I climbed onto my bed and sobbed all over again. God, I was pathetic.

* * *

I was startled awake by my bed dipping and strong arms wrapping around my waist. "It's me, Freckles."

I turned to face Reese and dropped my face into his chest. "What are you doing here?"

"You sounded like you were gonna have a nervous breakdown, baby. I had to do something."

I burst into tears and sobbed into his T-shirt.

"Hey now," he crooned, and lifted my chin. "What's goin' on, Lex?"

I squeezed my eyes shut tight. "I think I'm pregnant."

"Eyes, Lex."

I met his as I sniffed.

"You think you're pregnant?" he asked.

I nodded. "I'm sorry. I didn't think about the Pill, I mean, I did, but it's not like I can just show up at the doctor, but I didn't want to stop having sex, which was really selfish of me, because I shouldn't burden—"

"Baby, breathe."

I took a couple of deep breaths which really didn't help.

"Did you take a test?"

"No. But I'm late. Like three weeks late and you know me, I'm never late. And I'm puking my guts out, plus I'm yelling at everyone. I snapped at the Reverend Mother, Reese. Over fucking salami. I'm a monster."

He chuckled and pulled me closer. "Okay, baby, it's okay. I've got you."

"Why are you laughing?"

He stroked my cheek. "Because you're fuckin' adorable."

"I'm a whore," I rasped.

Reese grew serious. "What the fuck?"

"I'm an unmarried pregnant nun, Reese. What

other word is there?"

He wiped my tears from my cheeks and kissed me gently. "You're not a nun and you're not gonna be unmarried for long."

"Reese, we can't get married until the trial's over."

"Who says?" he challenged.

"Everyone."

"Do you say that?"

"Well…no."

"And I sure as hell don't say that," he said, stroking my cheek. "So, we'll get married tomorrow."

"But we can't live together."

"Sure we can."

"Reese, stop it," I hissed.

"Stop what?"

"Stop making promises you can't keep."

"I *can* keep them."

I blinked up at him. "What?"

"Got it all set, baby. Cullen's been working around the clock."

"Who's Cullen?"

"Cullen Wallace. Brother of one of the Dogs. Hatch. You'll meet him soon, probably," he explained. "Our house is fully wired, we have a panic room in the basement—"

"Since when?"

"Finished it yesterday, not that we'll need it, the home isn't in my name."

"Whose name is it in?"

"Private holding."

"So you hid it?"

"I hid it."

"That's kind of genius," I admitted.

"I'm aware, baby."

"What about a license?" I challenged.

"Got that sorted too."

"Without me?"

"Yeah, baby. I know people."

"I'm really sorry I got pregnant."

"Don't you dare apologize," he admonished. "Unless you're not happy…are you unhappy, Lex?"

"What? No," I countered. "Are you unhappy?"

"No, baby. I'm thrilled."

I leaned back a little. "Really?"

His hand slid to my belly. "A life we created is percolating in here, Lex. We made that. I love that…and you. I'm humbled you're gonna have my baby. Now, you gonna marry me?"

"When?"

"Tomorrow."

"I don't have a dress."

"Yes, you do."

I frowned. "I do?"

"Yep. Bought you one today."

"You did *not*."

"I did."

"But *I* wanted to pick my dress," I cried.

"You don't trust me?"

"I don't know," I hedged. "It's my wedding dress. You're not supposed to see it until I walk down the aisle."

He sighed. "I haven't."

"Well, that doesn't make sense! How the hell can you buy a dress if you don't know what you're buying?"

He smiled. "I took Paisley with me. She chose it, tried it on, without me seeing it, then picked your size."

"Oh," I whispered. "Paisley would know exactly what I wanted."

"It's why I took her."

"I can't believe you spent a day shopping with Paisley."

"Four."

"What?" I squeaked.

"Four days. We've been doing this dance for two weeks."

"What the hell?" I snapped. "I thought she was only allowed out to go to work."

"Technically she is, but Cameron arranged some protection." He sighed. "I thought she was fuckin' with me after the third store on day two, but she finally found it today and it's even the perfect size. Better be. Cost me a fuckin' fortune."

"Ohmigod, Reese, really?"

"Yeah, baby, really."

I snuggled closer. "I love you so much."

"Love you too. So…wedding. Tomorrow?"

"Yes, please."

"Okay, baby. It's all set. Father Michael's gonna marry us. Ryder and the crew will be here, as will Paisley. Can't get your mom out, I'm afraid—"

"It's okay. As long as Paisley's there, I'm okay. What about Sergei?"

"Still workin' on that."

"You are?"

"Do I know how close you are to your brother?" he challenged.

"Yes, you know how close I am to my brother," I grumbled.

"Then do you doubt I'd move heaven and earth to get him to his only sister's wedding?"

I bit my lip. “I don’t doubt it for a second.”

“Good.” He leaned forward and kissed me gently. “Then I am moving heaven and earth, Lex.”

“Thank you, honey.”

“My pleasure, baby.” He kissed me again. “I need to go.”

I wrapped my arms around him like a vice. “No.”

“I’m not supposed to be in here.”

“I don’t care.”

He pulled me close and kissed my forehead. “Okay, just a little longer.”

* * *

I awoke the next morning to an empty bed. I didn’t remember falling asleep and I certainly didn’t feel Reese leave me, but I was much calmer than I had been the day before.

On my nightstand were a plastic Fred Meyer bag and a note.

For your peace of mind, Freckles. I love you, R.

I peeked inside and found two pregnancy tests. I grabbed my phone and pressed call.

Reese answered immediately. “Hey, baby. You okay?”

“Are you sure you don’t want me to wait to take these with you?”

“Up to you.”

I sighed. “I thought you’d be jonesing to ‘share in this moment’ with me.”

He chuckled. “I’m tryin’ to give you some space, but, yeah, if you could wait, I’d appreciate it.”

“How soon can you be here?”

“We’re gettin’ married today, remember? Not comin’ ’til it’s time.”

I wrinkled my nose. "Okay, I can wait."

"Yeah?"

"Yes, honey. Of course."

"Okay, thanks."

I closed my eyes. I missed him…even though I'd just seen him.

"Hey," Reese whispered.

"Yeah?"

"I love you, baby. Can't wait to marry you."

"Me too, sugar bear."

"See you in two hours."

"What?" I squeaked, glancing at my clock. "That's not enough—"

"Knock, knock," Paisley called as she pushed open my door.

"Sounds like hair and makeup's there," Reese said.

"Honey, two hours is *not* enough time."

He chuckled. "I love you, baby. See you in one hour and fifty-six minutes."

He hung up.

I turned to Paisley who was laying a garment bag on my bed. "Hi."

She wrapped her arms around me and hugged me tight. "Hi."

"I can't believe you're doing this."

Paisley rolled her eyes. "I didn't have much choice. I couldn't let Reese pick your dress; you would have looked like some biker ho."

I giggled. "Well, I appreciate you having my back."

She shrugged. "It was easy, honestly. Reese bought me my bridesmaid's dress."

"He did?"

"Yep." She grinned. "He doesn't know he did, but he did."

I was pretty sure Reese *did* know he bought it, but I didn't say that to Paisley. She liked getting one over on people, so I let her have that.

"Okay, go shower," she instructed. "Don't wash your hair."

"I know the drill," I retorted, and hugged her again. "Thanks, bestie. I love you."

"Love you too."

I headed off to the bathroom, taking the quickest shower in history, and then I joined Paisley (and Sadie) back in my room to prepare for my wedding.

* * *

Paisley and I walked out to the foyer of the sanctuary and I couldn't stop a gasp as my brother walked toward me. He looked a little beat up, but he'd showered and wore a suit that appeared to have been made for him…and he was alive.

I made a run for him, but he stopped me before I could jump into his arms. "Can't mess up the dress, sis," he said with a chuckle, pulling me in for a gentle hug.

He was right. The dress was perfect. The lace top had capped sleeves, a low V-neck with a satin bow around the waist, and the lace flared over the top of a tulle skirt and floated down like a chain of flowers.

"Paisley nailed it, huh?" I said.

"You look beautiful." He glanced at Paisley. "As do you."

"Thanks, buddy," she said. And she did. Her ink blue a-line dress with halter neckline hugged every one of her curves and suited her coloring to a T. She'd nailed her choice as well.

I hugged him again and forced back tears. "I can't believe you're here."

"I know, *myshka*."

I rolled my eyes. He'd always called me "little mouse," mostly because he said I was the loudest human on the planet, so it was his affectionate attempt at irony.

Stroking my cheek, he smiled. "But I don't have long and Reese is waiting."

I nodded. Paisley handed me a bouquet of light pink and white roses and baby's breath, and I slipped my hand into the crook of Sergei's arm. It was time. I couldn't believe it. After all this time, Reese was mine until death…because divorce wasn't an option… death would come first.

I bit back a smile as Sergei walked me into the church just as the music started to play. He leaned down and kissed my cheek and Paisley stepped around us and strolled toward the aisle.

"Ready?" Sergei whispered.

I nodded and we began our walk toward my future.

* * *

Reese

Alexa came into view and any breath left in my body disappeared. God damn, she was beautiful. Her eyes met mine and I could see the tears threatening to spill…hell, I was biting back my own.

The tip of her tongue touched her lips and I wanted to forget all the ceremony bullshit and take her into a side room and fuck her senseless, especially when she gave me a slow, sexy smile. Unfortunately, the chapel was filled with a dozen or so bikers, at least twenty nuns, and a priest. Not a group of people I could ditch without being noticed…not to mention the fact it was my wedding day.

Hey, baby, I mouthed to her as she moved toward me.

Hi, she mouthed back.

Sergei delivered Alexa to me and I lifted her hand to my mouth, kissing her palm. "You are stunning," I whispered.

"So are you," she whispered back.

I wore black jeans, motorcycle boots and a white button up, but I'd dressed up the ensemble with a black dinner jacket.

Father Michael led us through our vows (not fast enough in my opinion) and then it was finally time to kiss my wife.

Fuck.

My wife.

Alexa stared up at me with a watery smile as I cupped her face. "Hi, wife."

"Well, hello there, husband."

I leaned down and gently kissed her. She opened her mouth to deepen the kiss, but I kept our first kiss as a married couple PG-13…and saw her irritation all over her face. I smiled and turned her to face our friends as Father Michael introduced us.

I took Alexa's hand and kissed it gently, raising an eyebrow at her expression. "Patience, Mrs. Alden."

"You know how I feel about patience, Mr. Alden."

I grinned. "Smile, Lex, you just got married…to me."

She finally smiled and faced our friends.

Alexa

I WAS MARRIED. I couldn't remember a time I'd been happier. I *wasn't* happy, however, that I couldn't strip my man…my *husband*…naked and jump on his cock in the middle of the church, but that would probably be frowned upon by the nuns.

Reese looked edible. He also smelled incredible. Man mixed with soap, leather, and a hint of cologne that was almost elusive. This was a problem for me. It had *always* been a problem for me.

As we walked down the aisle, I gripped his arm like a lifeline and went through the motions of greeting our friends and doling out the obligatory hugs, all the while, just wanting to strip Reese bare in order to lick every inch of him.

I was probably going to hell having these thoughts

in a church.

I sighed, earning yet another raised eyebrow from the old ball and chain.

"Patien—"

"If you say 'patience' one more time, you're going to lose a limb," I threatened.

"I highly doubt that," he countered with a chuckle. "You like all my limbs."

"Sugar bear?"

"Yeah?"

I crooked my finger so he'd come closer and I whispered for his ears only, "I want to get you somewhere I can suck your cock until you come so hard, you can't stand up. I need to know how many licks it takes to get to your gooey center, so to speak." He hissed through his teeth and I smiled. "Can you make that happen, honey?"

"Hell, yeah, I can make that happen."

"Excellent."

"But it's gonna have to wait a little bit."

I wrinkled my nose. "Well, that sucks."

He grinned. "Or doesn't as the case may be."

"Ohmigod, you're impossible."

"I'll make it up to you."

I smiled. "Can't wait."

"It's party time, but we should probably figure out if you can drink," he whispered once we made it to the foyer. The rest of our friends were still milling about the church.

I nodded. "I took the test, but I haven't looked at it."

"I thought you were going to wait for me."

I shrugged. "I figured everyone would be around, so I did my thing and it's in a zippy in my purse."

"Where's your purse?"

"Paisley has it."

"Okay, why don't we get that from her now and look, sound good?"

I smiled. "Eager beaver, sugar bear?"

He chuckled. "You found me out."

"Let's refresh your makeup, Lex," Paisley said as she approached, handing me my purse.

"Sounds good."

"Actually, can you give us a minute?" Reese asked.

"Sure."

Reese guided me into the bathroom off the foyer and locked the door behind us.

"What if someone needs to use that, honey?"

He grinned. "We won't be long. Grab the stick."

"So romantic." I handed him my bouquet and dug in my purse for the pregnancy test. Pulling it out, I set my purse on the counter and pulled the test out of the baggie.

Reese wrapped an arm around my waist and kissed my temple.

"Ready?" I asked.

He nodded and I held up the test…and suddenly felt an overwhelming feeling of disappointment. It was negative.

"Oh," I whispered.

"Are you okay?"

I shrugged. "I don't know," I admitted. "I really want to have your baby."

Reese smiled. "And you will."

"But I want to be pregnant now."

He chuckled. "Then I'm gonna have to work hard to make that happen on our honeymoon, huh?"

I sighed. "It's not a good time."

"Why not?"

"Oh, I don't know…I'm testifying against a couple of the most dangerous people in the world, etcetera, etcetera."

"Well, for now, you and I are heading up to Mt. Hood, so we'll have a week of uninterrupted baby making time where you'll be safe."

"We're going skiing?" I whispered, grabbing the lapels of his jacket.

"If you want to ski, we can ski."

"I'm more of a drink-hot-toddies-by-the-fire kind of girl."

"You don't say," he deadpanned.

I smiled. "You remembered."

"I remember everything when it comes to you."

"Apparently." I stood on my tiptoes and kissed him gently. "I love you."

"I love you too."

"You look amazing."

"So do you." He slid his hands to my waist. "You are the most beautiful woman on the planet."

"Thank you for the dress, Reese," I said. "You nailed it."

"Paisley nailed it."

"You thought to get Paisley involved, so *you* nailed it."

He grinned. "You're welcome."

"When do we leave?"

"We're heading up there tomorrow. Got somethin' else planned tonight."

"So this is operation: give Alexa the most perfect wedding and honeymoon on the planet."

Reese stroked my face. "Is it working?"

"Yeah, honey, it's working beautifully." I blinked back tears. "Thank you. For everything. But most of all, thank you for loving me."

"That's the easy part."

I leaned back to meet his eyes and raised an eyebrow.

"What?" he challenged. "It's easy to love you, Lex. But when I get you riled up, you tend to use fuck in various and creative ways, and you know what your dirty mouth does to me."

"This is why you piss me off?"

"Absolutely."

"Fuck," I whispered.

He groaned. "See?"

I giggled. "I'm gonna snack on your fuckin' cock later. I'm going to pretend it's a lollipop."

"Lex, stop," he hissed.

"Stop what, honey?" I asked, sliding my hand under the waistband of his jeans. "Wow. You're so fuckin' hard."

His mouth landed on mine so hard, he almost bruised me…deliciously so. He broke the kiss almost as quickly. "Shit!"

"Why did you stop?"

"Someone's bangin' on the door, baby."

He was right.

"Damn it," I whispered, and made my way to the locked door, opening it.

Paisley rolled her eyes and walked inside. "Time to freshen up. You two will need to wait for a bit for whatever you planned to do in here. With a church full of people. And thin walls."

"Don't you dare judge me," I demanded. "I've waited a long time for this and, *hello*, married."

"Which is when the sex dries up," Paisley retorted.

"Like hell it does," Reese said.

I giggled. "Yeah, I'm pretty sure that's not going to be a problem."

"Congratulations," Paisley droned. "Makeup."

"Right," I said, and ushered Reese out of the bathroom.

Paisley fixed my makeup and then it was time to party. I couldn't wait to get my drink on now that I knew I wasn't pregnant.

Since I was surprised by the wedding, and had to wait for the honeymoon, I decided I was just going to live in the moment. Reese had gotten everything right so far, so I was excited for what he had in store for us.

I stepped out of the bathroom and straight into Reese's arms. He kissed me gently and then led me to the reception area at the back of the abbey.

"Did you smear my lipstick?" I asked, smiling up at him.

"You look beautiful, Lex."

"You didn't answer my question." I giggled, pulling away so I could grab the compact out of my clutch. I fixed a tiny little smudge in the corner of my mouth, then slid the mirror back in my purse. "I can't believe you were going to let me go in there looking like that."

"I can do a better job if you want me to."

I slid my hand into the crook of his elbow. "Later."

"I'll hold you to that."

I grinned up at him and then Ryder announced us, and we walked in to applause and hoots. The rest of the night passed in a blur and then I was whisked away to the Sentinel in downtown Portland.

Reese had booked a lovely room with its own terrace, where we could see the city lights considering it was a beautifully clear night.

"Reese, this is amazing," I breathed out as I stared across Portland.

He handed me a glass of wine and kissed my shoulder before wrapping an arm around my waist. "Yeah, it is. Kinda wish we were staying here."

"Mt. Hood'll be gorgeous."

"Yep, got a few other things planned as well."

"What?" I asked.

"Not telling."

I giggled. "Bet I can make you tell me."

He kissed me. "You can try."

"Challenge accepted."

Reese laughed and we headed back inside. He took my wine, set it on the nightstand, and unzipped my wedding dress, holding it so it wouldn't pool on the floor. I stepped out of it, and he lovingly laid it over a chair before rushing me and dropping me on the bed. "Fuckin' gorgeous."

I giggled. "You barely looked at me. I wore white just for you."

I had white lacy thigh highs with white, lace panties, and a barely there, strapless bustier. Since I had no time to react, I still wore my heels, and when I moved to take them off, Reese stopped me.

"Leave 'em on, baby." I nodded and he tugged the cups of the bustier down, releasing my breasts and sucked a nipple into his mouth. "I like you like this."

I arched into him. "Yeah?"

"Gorgeous, baby."

He rolled a nipple between his fingers and the sensation shot to my clit. I gasped and wrapped my legs around his waist, pushing my pussy against his already hard cock. He moved his lips to my neck and then slid back down to my breasts, kissing his way down my belly.

I sighed. "Reese?"

"Yeah, baby?"

"My turn next, okay?"

He grinned, removing the rest of his clothes. "Absolutely."

I grasped the headboard as he gave a quick and gentle suck on my clit, before moving his thumb into place to finish the job. What the man could do with his tongue was out of this world.

My climax came fast and hard, but I didn't take too much time to enjoy it. It was my turn after all, so I pushed Reese onto his back and slid my mouth over his cock. Wrapping my hand around the base and lowering my mouth onto him again, Reese dropped his head back onto the pillows. "Holy shit."

I couldn't help but grin. Reese's body always responded to me immediately, his breathing quickened as his hands pressed into my hair and his hips pitched up.

"Babe," he rasped, his body locking.

"Come," I mumbled against him.

He groaned as his orgasm rocked his body. I didn't move for several seconds before giving his cock one last kiss and then sliding up his body.

"Six licks," I said.

"Huh?" he rasped.

"To get to your center."

Reese laughed. "Should probably work on making it last longer."

"Nope, I'm good. You do you, booboo."

He chuckled again and rolled me onto my back where he promptly slid into me, and wove his fingers with mine, pushing my hands above my head.

"Harder," I ordered.

He slammed into me and I arched up to meet every thrust. Just before my climax hit, he released my hands and I gripped his head, guiding him to meet my kisses.

His tongue moved in my mouth at the same rate as his cock inside of me, then he slid his hand between us and fingered my clit and I broke, crying out as I shattered around him.

He thrust one more time and then I felt him pulse against my walls before kissing me again and kissing my neck. "Love you."

"I love you, too," I whispered, and we spent the next few hours exploring each other's bodies as husband and wife.

Alexa

THE NEXT AFTERNOON, we arrived at Timberline. Admittedly, the view was stunning, but all I could think about was the Shining. All that appeared to be missing was the creepy hedge maze.

All work and no play makes Lex a dull girl.

It wasn't lost on me that Reese checked us in under a different name…and I had to wear the stupid black wig, but I said nothing until we were alone in our room.

"Not taking any chances," he said, once we were behind the safety of the locked door.

"Am I going to have to wear the wig if we ski?"

"Yeah, baby, you are."

I sighed…dramatically. "I hate that thing."

"So do I." He smiled. "But look at it this way. You'll be alive…and well-bedded."

"But—"

"Gonna fuck you now, Freckles."

"Reese."

"You gonna give me grief?" he challenged.

"I—"

"*Alexa.*"

"I'll allow it." This certainly beat arguing so I licked my lips and looped my arms around his neck. "But you better make sure you do it hard."

I'd worn a long, slinky dress that was both comfortable and sexy, and Reese lifted it over my head within seconds. I was naked underneath, which earned me a hiss of surprise from his sexy mouth.

"You like that, huh?"

"Yeah, baby, I fuckin' love it." He kissed my neck as he cupped my breasts. "Probably good I didn't know about this while we were driving up."

"Probably." I tugged at his jeans, unzipping them and shoving them down his hips. "You gonna let me figure out how many more licks it takes—?"

"No way in hell," he interrupted.

I sighed. "I didn't think so."

"But I'll fuck you 'til you scream, then you can play the Tootsie Pop game again."

I giggled. "Deal."

He divested himself of the rest of his clothes and then lifted me onto the bed, tugging me to the edge of the mattress and burying his face between my legs. I slid my ankles over his shoulders and lifted my hips to get my pussy closer to his mouth.

"Wifey's got an insatiable cunt," Reese breathed out, then sucked my clit until I whimpered with need.

"Hubby's not going fast enough," I complained, and he chuckled.

He shifted and slid slowly into me. "Better?"

I nodded and he gripped my thighs and pulled me closer to anchor me to his body as he slammed into me. He touched me in no other way…just held me still as he buried himself inside of me. It drove me crazy…in a very irritating way.

"Reese," I whispered, panting to catch my breath.

"Don't come, baby."

"Since you're not messin' with my tits, I probably *won't*," I snapped.

This earned me a slap on my ass and I almost lost my mind.

"I said, don't come," he growled.

He had me pinned so I couldn't really move without having to break our connection…which of course was exactly what he wanted. "Reese. Please, baby."

He continued to slam into me, then his thumb went to my clit. "Now, Lex."

My walls tightened around his cock and I cried out his name as my climax rocked me to the core. Reese released my shaking legs and pulled gently out of me. "Next time I'll make sure I fuck with your tits…you know, since you can't come unless I do."

I shrugged. "I totally faked it."

"Your body didn't fake it."

"You don't think?"

He leaned down to kiss me. "Soaked my cock, baby."

"Bad vagina," I admonished, then giggled as he strolled to the bathroom, bringing back a warm washcloth to clean me up. "I think you just put a baby in me."

"Yeah? With my baby juice?" He threw the wash-cloth in the corner and stretched out beside me.

I groaned. "Gross, Reese."

"Splooge?"

"Ohmigod. No."

"Jizz?"

I began to laugh uncontrollably. "Stop! For the love of God, no."

"Baby batter?" He slid his arm around my waist and rolled me toward him.

I squealed with laughter as he continued.

"Baby gravy? Man-yonaise?

"Stop, stop," I begged. "I can't suck you off if I'm imagining swallowing man-yonaise."

"But you *love* man-yonaise." He shoved his face in the crook of my neck and rubbed his stubble over my skin, tickling me.

"I love *your* man-yon—ohmigod, no, I will *not* say it."

Reese ran his tongue over my collarbone, then kissed his way down to my breasts, drawing a nipple into his mouth gently. My laughter was quickly replaced with desire and I sighed as I arched against his mouth.

Linking his fingers with mine and stretching my arms above my head, Reese hovered above me and kissed me deeply before sliding into me slowly.

I wrapped my legs around his waist and bit his lower lip.

"You feelin' feisty?" he asked, pulling away with a hiss.

"If by feisty you mean horny, then, yes." I contracted my walls around his cock and his eyes closed briefly. "You gonna work the girls?"

He grinned. “You gonna do those kegel things again?”

I contracted again and he buried himself deeper.

“Fuck!” he breathed out, then released my hands so he could cup my breasts and twist my nipples into pebbles.

“Yes,” I rasped.

“On your knees, Lex,” he demanded, and I complied immediately.

“Can you keep yourself from coming, baby?” Reese slid into me and leaned forward to work my nipples again.

I licked my lips. “Probably not.”

He chuckled, slapping my bottom, and I dropped my head back with a gasp. “Ohmigod.”

“You wanna come then do this again?”

“Yes, yes I do,” I panted out.

This earned me another slap and I whimpered, but when one hand went to my clit and he slammed into me while he slapped me again, I exploded. He gave me a second to relish the feeling before he started all over again.

“Reese,” I breathed out as he buried himself inside of me again.

“Harder, baby?”

“Ohmigod, do you have to ask?”

He chuckled, giving me a soft smack before grabbing my hips and slamming into me over and over again. My body betrayed me, but luckily, Reese was right behind me. I cried out as I came, his cock pulsing inside of me, and we fell onto the mattress together.

“I love you,” he whispered, kissing my shoulder.

I smiled. “I love you, too, honey.”

“I have something to tell you.”

“That doesn’t sound good,” I said, and rolled to face him.

He smiled and cupped my face. “We’re not alone here.”

I sighed. “What do you mean we’re not alone?”

“Don’t worry, we’re alone, just not alone, alone.”

“Ohmigod, Reese, spit it out.”

“Got a couple guys and their women comin’ for cover.”

I sighed. “Will we see them?”

“Only if we want to.”

“I’m okay with that, in theory.”

Reese chuckled.

“Who are these people?” I asked.

“Hawk, he’s a Dog, and his wife, Payton. Her brother’s FBI and she’s good with a gun—”

“Are you now with this Dogs club? Out of one gang into another?”

“No, baby. And they’re not a gang. They’re legit and clean.”

“Is that it?”

“No,” he said. “Dallas and Macey’ll be here too. He’s FBI, she’s Payton’s best friend. Dallas figured out a way for them to be here as protection.”

I smacked his chest playfully. “As long as they’re not in our room with us, I’m good.”

“Never been one to invite people into our bed, baby.”

I giggled. “Hard no for me on that one.”

“Same.”

I kissed him gently. “This is why I like you.” My phone buzzed and I reached over and glanced at the screen. “Ohmigod.”

“What?”

"Roses for Anna has a show tonight. In Portland."

"Hard no for me," he said, and headed to the bathroom.

I groaned and flopped back onto the pillows. "F.Y. information, this sucks."

He walked back into the room and leaned down to kiss me quickly. "Did you really want to drive all the way back into the city?"

"No, not really," I admitted. "But I like the idea of being able to if we wanted to."

"I know, baby. It's not gonna be like this forever. Once you testify, things'll die down."

"*Then* can we go see Roses for Anna?"

He smiled. "Yes."

"What if they're only playing in, I don't know, Sweden?"

"Then I'll take you to Sweden."

I grinned. "Correct answer, husband."

"I'm aware, wife." He stretched out beside me again and kissed my shoulder. "Food or fucking?"

"Food," I said immediately.

"Are you sure?" His hand slid between my legs and cupped me.

I arched against his palm. "Why don't we order then you can make me come while we wait."

Reese chuckled. "I can do that."

* * *

The next morning, I donned the hated wig and we headed down to the lobby. As we walked to the restaurant for breakfast, I couldn't help but admire the breathtaking views. "It's beautiful, Reese."

He wrapped his arms around me and kissed me gently. "You wanna explore, or…"

"Or, what?"

"Go back to our room and fuck."

I giggled, stroking his face. "You're so romantic, Mr. Alden."

"Want you barefoot and pregnant, Mrs. Alden."

I laid my hand over his mouth. "Shh. People will hear you."

He chuckled. "Let's skip breakfast and—"

"No," I interrupted. "I'm starving."

"We can always order room service again."

"If I wasn't so hungry, and wanted all I can eat, I'd walk you right back to our room and keep doing what we've been doing," I admitted as Reese and I were led to our table.

He wrapped an arm around my waist and pulled me close, kissing my temple. "Rain check, then."

I smiled up at him. "Done."

We arrived at our table and I let out a quiet gasp. "What the heck?"

Ryder rose to his feet and Sadie craned her neck, letting out a quiet squeal as she stood as well. "Surprise," she said.

I looked up at Reese. "Did you know about this?"

"Nope." He grinned and led me to the table, hugging Ryder and Sadie, then waiting for me to do the same.

Sadie and I took our seats again and Ryder and Reese sat across from each other. "When did this all happen?" Reese asked, looping an arm over the back of my chair.

Ryder grinned. "You forget we know the same people."

"Sandy."

"Who's Sandy?" I asked.

"She works for us…specifically at the Brass Frog," Ryder said. "When Reese asked her to help with the travel stuff, I had her add me and Sadie to the list."

"Don't feel like you have to hang with us," Ryder said. "We're here for backup, not to interrupt your honeymoon. And if you want to eat alone, we won't be offended."

"I actually like the idea of getting to know each other a bit better," I said, and smiled.

Reese stroked my back. "I'm good with a standing dinner date. We'll play it by ear for the rest."

Ryder laughed. "Okay, brother."

"Are you saying you *don't* want us following you back to your room every night?" Sadie frowned at Ryder. "This is not what we agreed to, honey."

Reese chuckled. "Even though you're crashin' our honeymoon, I'm glad you're here, Sade, but the room thing is a hard no for me."

"Dang it," she breathed out, and I giggled.

I squeezed his knee. "Killjoy."

Our conversation was light and comical as we grabbed our food at the buffet, then sat down to eat. Sadie was an absolute hoot away from the abbey. She'd always been nice, but what I didn't pick up on before was her sense of humor. She was hilarious. Even Reese laughed (out loud) more than once and that just wasn't his style.

He and I had always had a good deal of laughter in our relationship, but he didn't engage with others the same way…and *never* with other women. Sadie was different and it was sweet the way Ryder watched her…totally besotted with her.

I couldn't blame him. I was starting to love her

too.

"You're going to have to roll me out of here," I complained taking one last bite of eggs.

"How about we suit up and build a snowman," Reese suggested.

I giggled. "Okay, Elsa."

Sadie grinned. "That sounds like so much fun."

"I'm in," I said.

"Good." Reese leaned in and whispered, "Maybe later I can show you what a real snowman does with his carrot."

We left our table and headed for our rooms. We changed into snow gear and met Ryder and Sadie back in the lobby. Just as we stepped outside, a tall, blond man sporting the sexiest handlebar moustache walked up to us, his arm wrapped around a gorgeous brunette.

"Hey, Hawk," Reese greeted. "Payton."

"Hi guys," Payton said.

Sadie pulled her in for a hug and I was introduced to the couple.

"Are you having fun?" Payton asked.

"Ask me once my breakfast has digested," I said, laying my hand over my stomach. "I think I might have eaten a little too much."

Payton giggled. "Then you should probably drink more coffee."

"You might be right," I agreed.

"Where are Dallas and Macey?" Reese asked.

"Macey's dealing with her motion sickness. She doesn't do well in cars, or planes, or boats, or trains," Payton said. "So, they went to their room."

"Oh, that sucks," I said. "I have some meclizine if she needs it."

"I'll check on her later and let you know if she needs anything," Payton said. "You'll meet her tomorrow, I'm sure."

"All's clear for the moment," Hawk said. "Dallas got the lodge guest list over to Brock, so he'll call if there are any red flags."

"Brock?" I asked.

"My brother," Payton said. "Dallas's partner."

"Oh, right." I remembered Reese giving me the lowdown on who everyone was, but there were so many people to keep track of. His sphere of influence had expanded greatly since we were young.

"Reese wants to build a snowman," Sadie said.

Hawk raised an eyebrow. "No shit?"

"No shit," Reese confirmed, and I giggled.

"Let's go," Payton said, and we headed around the corner, singing the song from Frozen and driving the men crazy.

Reese

I SLAMMED INTO Alexa and came harder than I ever had before. She was on all-fours, her perfect and luscious ass up, her cheek to the mattress, and I had just slapped her six times, giving her her second orgasm in as many minutes. Fuck me, I'd missed her.

"You're so tight."

"You keep doing what you're doing and you'll change that," she retorted, her voice breathless.

"Wasn't complaining, baby." I slid my palms across her back and cupped her ass. "Perfect."

"You can thank the sugar gods for that."

I chuckled. "You and your ice cream obsession."

"Mmm," she hummed.

I slid my finger through her wetness, my cock still encased in her tight, wet pussy. Moving my finger to her clit, I leaned forward and kissed her back, right where the rise of her ass met her spine.

"Reese," she whispered.

"More, baby?"

She pushed back against me trying to get closer and rasped, "Yes."

Running my finger through her wetness again, I slid it into her asshole and she mewed in need, pressing against me, so I slid in more.

"Baby," she whimpered.

"More?"

"Yes!"

I slammed into her, moving my finger as I moved my cock, and she exploded around me, collapsing on the bed, which meant I was forced to break contact with her ass or her pussy. I chose her ass, following her down and rolling us to our sides so I could continue to fuck her. I reached between her legs and cupped her mound, before focusing on her clit.

"Reese," she squeaked, another climax building.

One thing that hadn't changed since we'd been apart was her body's response to my touch. It was something I enjoyed as a teenager, but it was something I savored as a man. I had never loved a woman the way I loved her, and we may have been young when we fell for each other, but I knew my mind and my heart, and that was something that hadn't changed for me.

"Now, Lex."

Her pussy contracted around my throbbing cock and I held her close as I came hard inside of her.

Lex's body shook slightly and I kissed her shoulder. "You okay?"

"No," she sobbed.

I pulled out of her as gently as I could and rolled her to face me. "Baby? What the fuck? Did I hurt you?"

She shook her head, tears pouring down her face.

I frowned. "What's wrong?"

"I…I don't know."

I wiped her tears way and kissed her soft, wet lips. "It's okay, baby. I've got you."

"I can't ever lose you again," she ordered. "You have to promise me."

"I'm not going anywhere."

"Never."

"Never, baby. I love you. I *married* you. We're in it for life."

She licked her lips and nodded. "Swear."

"I swear." I stroked her cheek. "Not even death will separate us, Lex. If I die, I will haunt you like Patrick Swayze haunted Demi Moore."

"Not good enough."

"No?"

"No, you can't die. You have to promise to become a vampire instead."

"No."

"Why?" she challenged. "You don't have an aversion to blood…do you?"

"Blood's not a problem," I said. "Sparkling's where I draw the line."

She laughed so hard, she snorted, and I relaxed, pulling her in close again. "There's my girl."

"I love you," she said, still giggling.

"Love you more."

She dropped her head to my chest and sighed. "Thank you."

I stroked her back. "You're welcome."

"You know, this is the best day ever."

I chuckled and slid off the bed, heading for the shower. "Building a pornographic snow woman and then fucking like rabbits *is* pretty damn good."

Alexa leaned up on her elbows. "Where are you going?"

"Shower." I smiled. "Comin'?"

She gave me a slow grin. "Yes."

We made love several more times, getting dirty before getting clean again, then I took my wife back to bed. I didn't think I'd ever get used to finally having her soft body to hold all night long.

I moved my hand to her belly, sending every wish I had for a baby through my body. Fuck. A daughter, as beautiful as her mom, wreaking as much havoc on me was almost too much to hope for, but I hoped anyway.

This was my last coherent thought before I fell into oblivion.

* * *

Alexa

I was awoken by the ring of our room phone, then the quiet voice of Reese answering it.

"Yeah, man, no problem. Okay, see you in a bit." He hung up and leaned over me, kissing me gently.

"Who was that?" I asked, stretching.

"Dallas. Macey's really sick, so I need that motion sick stuff you brought."

I sat up and slid off the mattress. "The poor thing. That's the worst."

"I'll get 'em, honey, just direct me."

I smiled, kissing him gently. "I should get up anyway. Can't stay in bed all day when we have more lodge to explore."

I found the meclizine, threw on some clothes, and brushed my teeth just as a knock at our door came.

"Hey, Dal," Reese greeted. "Come on in. This is Alexa."

I grinned and shook Dallas's hand. Six-foot-two (same height as Reese), green eyes, dark hair with a tinge of red, he was really attractive and he looked really worried for his wife.

I shook some meclizine into a glass and handed it to him. "Macey's a nurse, right?"

Dallas nodded.

"Let her know these are meclizine, twelve-point-five milligrams."

He gave me a relieved smile. "She hoped you'd say that."

"Yeah?"

"Yeah. She figured since the drive wasn't that long, she'd be good. She wasn't."

I wrinkled my nose. "That sucks donkey balls."

He chuckled, tipping the glass toward me. "Thanks for this. We'll see you at dinner if these work."

"It was nice to meet you," I said, and Dallas left.

Reese wrapped his arms around me and stroked my hair. "How are you feelin'?"

"Good, honey. Perfect, actually."

"Yeah?"

"Yes." I grinned up at him. "Are you hungry?"

"For food or you?"

I giggled. "Both. But let's start with food."

He kissed me, gently biting my lower lip. "You

sure?"

"Nope," I retorted, and slid my hands under his shorts, pushing them down his hips.

Kneeling before him, I took his cock in my mouth. Just the tip to start, then sliding my lips half-way down.

"Lex?" he whispered.

I pulled away and looked up at him. "Shh. I'm hungry. Let me eat."

He grinned and I went back to my task. I gripped his length gently and pulled down as I took him into my mouth again. I ran a nail over his nipple, continuing to work his cock with my mouth and hand.

He threaded his fingers through my hair and gripped my scalp, his hips moving and fucking my mouth so effectively, I almost came right where I knelt.

"Now, baby."

I sucked a little harder, flattening my hands on his thighs as his body locked, and he came in my mouth. I waited until his hands left my head, and then I released his cock with a gentle smack, swallowing.

His hands slid under my arms and he lifted me onto the bed, dragging me to the edge and settling my ankles on his shoulders as he slammed into me.

I was anchored so tightly to his body, I had no range of motion in my lower extremities, so I gripped the bedding and held on while he worked my body with an expertise that always left me shaking…in a good way.

"Reese!" I rasped as my climax crested.

"Don't come," he growled.

I clamped my walls around him and he let out a grunt.

"Fuck!"

"Not so easy, huh?" I quipped, and he grinned down at me.

"Minx."

He released my legs and I wrapped them around his waist as he hovered over me and kissed me. His hips slowed and I pulled him closer with my legs, lifting my hips to take him deeper.

"Your pussy's insatiable."

I grinned, nodding. "Your fault."

"Glad, baby."

"Me too, sugar bear."

His hand slid between us and he fingered my clit as he continued to bury himself inside of me. "Now, Lex."

I wasn't quite ready, and he seemed to guess that, so he continued to move and work my clit until I exploded around him.

I kissed him deeply and stroked his stubbled cheek. "If that didn't put a baby in me, nothing will."

Reese laughed and we got dressed and headed out to feed our other appetite.

* * *

Macey was in fact feeling well enough to join us for dinner, and our waiter set up a table for eight.

"That meclizine saved me," Macey said, hugging me before taking her seat. "Thank you so much."

"You're welcome," I said.

Macey was stunning…model stunning, with long dark-auburn hair, and she had everyone's notice as she walked by. Watching her and Payton made me miss Paisley, which Reese must have picked up on, because he leaned over as though to kiss my cheek, whispering, "What's wrong?" instead.

I smiled and squeezed his knee. "I'm okay. Just missing Paisley."

He kissed my cheek then and studied me.

"I'm good," I said. "Promise."

"Love you, Lex."

"Love you, too." I kissed him gently and shook off my blues.

We were heading up the hill in the morning, so we turned in much sooner than we normally would have and I slept snuggled close to my man until it was time to wake up.

Sort of.

At some point, in what I assumed was the middle of the night, I awoke to an empty bed. I didn't think anything of it until Reese was gone longer than he should have been.

"Reese?"

No answer, so I climbed out of bed and was just pulling on a pair of shorts when he walked back into the room. "Where have you been?"

He grinned. "Needed some extra towels."

"It's not that urgent, is it?" I challenged. "We could always call in the morning."

"You're here to be spoiled, baby."

"I can't argue with that." I smiled, sliding my shorts back off. "Since you're awake, I require some attention."

He chuckled, removing his clothing. "I'm here to serve."

Alexa

THE ALARM SOUNDED far too soon for my liking and then as soon as we were up and getting dressed, our breakfast arrived.

"I think you broke my vagina." I sat at our little desk and took a bite of bacon.

Reese laughed as he poured us coffee. "Sorry not sorry."

I grinned. "Not complaining."

"Glad to hear it."

"Are we meeting everyone here?"

"Yeah." Reese checked his watch. "In about ten minutes."

"What?" I squeaked, standing. "I'm not ready."

"Maybe if someone had gotten up when I woke her…"

"Maybe if someone hadn't broken my vagina," I retorted.

Reese laughed again and smacked my bottom. "You look gorgeous."

"I have no makeup on."

"So?"

"So, you're prettier than I am."

Reese frowned. "Are you high?"

I slapped on some tinted moisturizer and blush, but found myself pushed onto the bed gently. "Take it back."

I sighed. "Sugar bear, I need to finish."

He straddled me and his hands hovered over my stomach. "You can…when you take it back."

"I can't take it back. You *are* prettier than me," I said. "Have you looked in a mirror?"

His hands connected with my stomach and I squealed with laughter.

"Reese! I'm going to pee."

"Take it back."

"No."

More tickling.

"Reese!"

"You know the deal, Lex."

"Okay, okay, I take it back. I'm totally hotter than you are."

He grinned, leaning down to kiss me gently. "Thank you."

I smacked his chest fisting his shirt in my hand. "You're ridiculous."

"But I'm not wrong." He slid off the bed and pulled me up. "You've got about five minutes."

"You're gonna need to let me go, honey."

"One thing first."

He kissed me…deeply…which left me struggling to catch my breath as I went back to my task. "Not fair, sugar bear."

"Did you learn your lesson?"

I giggled. "Maybe, maybe not."

He kissed me again. "Do you need another lesson?"

I nodded. "Yes, but let's put a pin in it until we get back. Then, there better be spanking."

"I can make that happen."

I grinned and finished my makeup, pulling my hair back in a ponytail, having been assured I didn't have to wear the dreaded wig again since I'd have a helmet while we skied.

A knock at our door came and we met Ryder and Sadie in the hallway, then joined Dallas, Macey, Hawk, and Payton at the elevators.

I was a bundle of excited energy and I gripped Reese's hand as we headed out for our excursion. I'd never been skiing, so heading into the "wilderness" was super exciting for me…even if it was labeled the "bunny hill."

Reese had organized a picnic on the hill with more food than we could eat, including crab and lobster. I nearly stuffed myself sick because you get me anywhere near shellfish and I will eat all of it. Every single delicious morsel.

I was very glad we didn't have to walk far after eating…I'm pretty sure Reese would have had to roll me back to our room.

"I think I may have gained twenty pounds," Payton complained as we sat down to remove our gear.

We'd skied down the slight hill, right up to the

lodge and then handed our skis and boots to the attendant.

Hawk chuckled. "I'm good with that."

I leaned heavily against Reese and he looped an arm around my waist, kissing my temple. "You good?"

I smiled up at him. "I'm perfect."

"That's what I want to hear."

"Are you always going to be like this?" I asked.

"Like what?"

"All sweet and amiable and crap."

"Sweet and amiable and *crap*?"

I giggled. "Yes. I like it."

"I'll endeavor to continue to make you happy."

"Never mind."

"What?"

"I take it back." I wrinkled my nose. "Don't 'endeavor' to do anything."

He cocked his head. "Why?"

"Um, because if you're super nice and never ornery, I won't get good sex," I whispered.

Reese laughed so hard, our friends all turned to study him.

"What? Nice guys can't give good sex?" he challenged.

"No…nice guys hump."

"Ohmigod, they so do," Payton agreed.

"*Hump*?" Reese asked.

"Yes. Real men know how to satisfy a woman, but nice guys only know how to hump," I said. "Humping occurs only on the appointed night of the week, and only missionary style is sanctioned."

"You don't say," Hawk said, trying to keep his laughter at bay.

"I agree," Macey piped in.

"It's a strictly lights off, socks on affair," I continued.

Sadie giggled so hard, she snorted.

"And your so-called 'ornery' men?" Reese asked.

"They do whatever it takes."

He raised an eyebrow. "Meaning?"

"Well, you know the difference between sensual and kinky, right?"

"Do tell?" he asked.

"Sensual is when you bring a feather to bed," I said.

"I can't believe I'm going to ask this," Sadie said, her cheeks pink. "But what about kinky?"

"You bring the whole damn bird," Hawk supplied.

"Spoken like a real man," Payton said.

"I'd be a little nervous about the bird flu," Sadie said.

"Always bag your beak," Dallas retorted.

We all dissolved into laughter and Reese pulled me closer.

Arriving back inside the lodge, we headed to our room and got ready for dinner. Despite my pig-out fest, I was starving again, but I took extra care with my appearance, knowing Reese would look hot as usual.

And I wasn't wrong. He wore dark jeans and a black button up with a paisley tie, his black cowboy boots, and a black vest. He'd swept his unruly hair away from his face and he was edible.

"You okay?" he asked, his mouth turned up in a half smile.

"Other than wanting to strip you down and lick every inch of your body, yep, I'm great."

He chuckled. "Back atya."

I smiled. I wore the little black cocktail dress he'd bought me, accessorizing with a blingy, crystal belt and strappy, heeled silver sandals. "I have nothing on underneath, just in case you want to take advantage of that later."

"Fuck, baby, don't say shit like that."

I giggled, glancing at his growing erection. "Need me to take care of that?"

He dropped his head back and counted to ten. "Nope, I'm good."

I rolled my eyes and grabbed my purse and room key. "Ready?"

"Yeah, baby, but first…" he leaned down and kissed me sweetly. "You look beautiful."

"Thank you. So do you."

He took my hand and we walked (quickly) to the elevator and then into the dining room. I really was hungry, but when we approached our table, there were two people sitting there I didn't recognize. Their backs were turned toward us, so I frowned up at Reese and he smiled.

"What?" I asked.

"Lex," Paisley called, and I realized the couple weren't strangers, but Paisley and my brother.

"What did you do?" I squeaked, squeezing Reese's hand.

"Go say hi," he ordered, nodding toward them.

I made a run for Paisley, pulling her in for a hug, then Sergei. "What are you guys doing *here*?"

Paisley giggled. "Reese set it up. Sergei and I drove up this afternoon."

"It's apparently not typically kosher to crash someone's honeymoon," Sergei said. "But Reese made it happen."

I pulled Reese in for a hug. "Thank you."

He kissed my temple. "You're welcome."

The rest of the group arrived and Dallas, Macey, Hawk, and Payton offered to sit at a table close by so we could catch up. After another fabulous meal, we headed to the bar for dancing and drinks. After more than a few too many, Reese took me (carried me) back to our room and lovingly undressed me, mostly because I couldn't.

* * *

Reese

"I can't believe you did that," Alexa said.

I chuckled, undoing her sandals and throwing them in the closet. Lex was close to drunk, and cute as hell.

"Why is that funny?" she demanded.

"Because you're always surprised when I do nice things for you."

She wrinkled her nose. "Am I?"

I smiled, unzipping her dress. "A little."

She stopped me from pulling her dress off, grabbing my hands. "I'm really sorry, honey."

"It's fine, baby."

"No, it's not," she countered, bursting into tears. "I'm a *monster*."

I settled her on the edge of the bed and knelt between her legs. "Baby, you are *not* a monster."

"I am," she wailed. "You do nice things for me all the time and I take them for granted."

Well, she'd gone down the wasted highway. "Lex."

"What?" She sniffed and then hiccupped.

I bit back a chuckle, 'cause she was so fuckin' cute. "I love you."

She threw her arms up. "Well, you shouldn't. I'm horrible."

"Okay, baby, up," I directed, pulling her off the bed and sliding her dress off her shoulders. I had to force myself not to react, considering she was, in fact, completely naked under her dress. "I think it's time for you to sleep it off."

"Are you going to leave me?"

"What the fuck?"

"You should. I'm no good for you," she slurred.

I lost my battle with my laughter and pulled her close. "I'm never leaving you, Alexa. Now, time for bed."

She kissed my neck. "I love you so much, Reese."

"I love you too, honey."

I caught her just as she went limp and grinned as I gently tucked her into bed, totally oblivious and snoring louder than my old bulldog.

While she slept, I undressed, then climbed in beside her pulling her close and kissing her gently. She moaned, responding to me even in her sleep. I wrapped myself around her and let myself fall into oblivion.

* * *

I awoke, rock hard. Especially considering soft, firm lips were kissing their way down my body to my cock. "Someone's awake."

Alexa giggled. "Well, I didn't get a chance to thank you properly for tonight."

"Continue with your gratefulness, baby. Don't let

me stop you."

She wrapped her mouth around my cock again and took me deep in her throat. I drew my knees up and wrapped her hair around my hand, tugging gently. With her tongue pressed to the underside of my cock, she took me deeper and I groaned as she gripped the length and pulled down with her hand.

"Fuck, Lex."

She moved her mouth with her hand, and I loosened my grip on her hair. She squeezed my thigh and released my dick. "Don't."

"Don't what?"

"Don't you dare interrupt me."

"I wasn—"

"The second you let go of my hair, it indicated to me you may be inclined to drag me into a position where you can shove your cock into my pussy," she informed me. "I have no problem with this. But not right now. Right now, I'm enjoying myself. I will let you fuck me when I'm done, but if you don't come in my mouth and give me the high protein breakfast my body is craving, I'll be really pissed."

I chuckled. "I wouldn't dare. Continue."

She went back to her task, cupping my balls and moving her hand faster, then gripping me harder.

"Fuck," I whispered. She worked me faster and I felt my sac tighten. "Lex," I hissed. "Now."

I exploded into her mouth and she squeezed me gently before releasing my dick and smiling up at me.

"Now, that's a tasty breakfast," she said, doing her best Jules from Pulp Fiction impersonation.

"Yeah? You like those jizz-eos, huh?"

"Is the mascot, Captain Cum Shot?" she lobbed back.

I laughed, pulling her up my body and kissing her deeply. "Fuck me, I love you."

"I love you too." She flopped on her back and spread her arms and legs, taking a deep breath. "You may take me now."

I grinned and took what she was offering.

Alexa

MY HEART WAS light as I walked with Reese up to the covered pool area. The group was meeting there to hang out and eat lunch.

We had another ski excursion the next day, but for now, it was a free day, and I had all my favorite people surrounding me.

Sergei was already in the pool, flirting with a really cute blonde, so I waved and headed to where Paisley was lounging next to Macey with Sadie on the end, looking to be very asleep, under a propane heater away from the water. Paisley stood and pulled me in for a hug.

"Ohmigod," I breathed out. "I love your suit."

Paisley had a bubbly and confident personality

and she currently wore a one-piece fifties style swimsuit that fit her personality perfectly. It was low-cut with all manner of fruit in the pattern. She'd wrapped a sarong over her waist to hide her "thunder thighs" as she called them (I personally thought she had a figure to die for, but as women, we always found fault with our own bodies). She also wore a heavy winter coat…it was still quite cold, even with the heat pumping in through the vents. She and I were very similar in coloring, so much so, people often mistook us for sisters, which we never corrected. Where the similarities ended, however, was she was petite and curvy, and I was five-foot-seven with a more athletic stature…other than my boobs. I'd been blessed with a full C-cup. Paisley, however, double D's all the way.

"I love yours too," she said, with a cheeky grin.

"Don't think I don't know that was your doing," I retorted.

Reese had let me know that Paisley helped pack my bag for this excursion, which also meant her choosing a few items (like my bikini), which looked great on me, but was far more revealing than I would have picked.

Reese wrapped his arms around me from behind. "I wholeheartedly approve of the bikini, baby."

I snorted. "You would."

"I'm gonna go talk to the guys for a bit."

I smiled up at him. "Take your time."

He kissed me gently and left me with Paisley and Macey. "Where's Payton?"

"She went to grab something from their room," Macey provided.

"I say let's get in the hot tub."

Paisley nodded, so us girls climbed into the hot

water and I leaned my back against the stone. "So when did all of this"—I waved my hands between Paisley and Sergei—"take place?"

"Reese called us the night before last." Paisley grinned. "I don't want to know what it cost him, but he made it happen."

"Ohmigod, he paid too?"

"Yep."

I blinked back tears and looked over at Reese who turned toward me and smiled. I mouthed, *I love you.* He smiled wider and gave me a chin lift, then turned back to Dallas, Ryder, and Hawk.

"Are those tears happy or sad?" Paisley asked.

I reached over and squeezed her hand. "Definitely happy, honey."

Cold water sprayed over me and I squealed, sitting up quickly. "Sergei!" I snapped.

He was shaking his wet head and laughing like an idiot. He grabbed his towel and leaned down to kiss my cheek. "Your husband's pretty cool, sis."

I smiled up at him. "I'm aware."

He climbed into the hot tub beside me.

"Who's the cutie?" I asked.

"Her name is Tessa and she's here with her family."

"Is she legal?" Paisley challenged.

"Nineteen," he said.

"So, barely," she mused. "Just your type."

He chuckled. "Not plannin' on doin' anything but have a little fun, Pa."

"Well, don't hurt her, Ma, or you and I'll have a conversation."

I smiled and shook my head. Sergei had started

calling Paisley “Pa” back in high school, so she’d followed it up with “Ma.” Their nicknames had stuck and I knew Sergei loved it. Probably because he still had a massive crush on my best friend…which Paisley still didn’t reciprocate.

“Alex!”

I turned toward the frantic sound of Payton’s voice as she rushed toward the guys’ huddle. Alex was Hawk’s real name, and he’d mentioned she only used it when she was really horny or scared. He’d received a fist to his shoulder from Payton for that tidbit of information, but since she looked scared, he pulled her close and studied her. They were a little too far away for me to hear everything, but I did get snippets.

“What the fuck?” he snapped.

Payton nodded over at me and then looked back up at him. Well, this was interesting.

I climbed out of the hot tub, shivering as I headed toward the men. I wrapped my arm around Reese’s waist and frowning up at him. “What’s going on?”

“Not sure, baby.”

“No,” Payton said, and grabbed Hawk’s arm. “He’s gone. If I see him again, I’ll let you know.”

“No, you’re never goin’ anywhere without me, so you won’t need to let me know shit.”

She nodded, dropping her head to his chest and wrapping her arms around his waist. After a few seconds, she pushed away from her husband and smiled. “I’m good, handsome.”

“Are you sure?”

She nodded. Macey wrapped an arm around her and led her to the hot tub. Sergei got the hint he should probably make himself scarce and I climbed back into the water. “What happened?” I asked.

"Some guy just attacked me in the hallway."

"What the hell?" Macey snapped.

"It's okay, I maced him."

Macey gave her a puzzled look. "You maced him and that makes this all okay? What the heck happened Payton? Spill!"

"I went back to our room to grab my sun block."

"Sun block. Really?" Macey said, her tone one of disbelief.

"Yes," Payton said again.

"There's no sun," I pointed out.

"There's still UV rays," Payton said. "Ergo, sun block needed."

"You mean sun *glock*," Macey retorted. "What's the SPF on that? 9mm?"

Payton rolled her eyes.

"You have a *gun* with you?" Sadie whispered.

"They're here to protect me," I pointed out. "So, it would make sense. I just didn't think any of you ladies would be packing."

"Oh, she's the only one who is," Macey said. "I hate…um…sun block."

Payton nodded. "Anyway, I grabbed my sun *block* and left my room. Some guy grabbed me from behind and tried to drag me into a room down the hall. I was able to fight my way out of his hold and mace him, then I just ran."

"Why didn't you just *squirt* him with the sun block?" Macey asked.

Payton sighed. "I'm not going to *squirt* the man in a crowded hotel, Macey."

I saw movement behind Payton and nodded. "It looks like Hawk's going somewhere."

"What?" Payton looked over her shoulder. "Shit.

He's going to blow this whole thing."

She climbed out of the water, grabbed a jacket and rushed after him."

"What would he blow?" Paisley asked.

"The guys are here mostly to cover me and Reese in case someone managed to find us," I explained. "If Hawk goes after this guy, it might scare anyone else into hiding. Reese wants them all eliminated."

"Or it could just be some creeper and not related to you at all," Macey provided.

"Probably," I agreed.

"I don't like this," Paisley said.

"You never like anything," I retorted. "You're practically a conspiracy theorist."

"Doesn't mean I don't know what I'm talking about."

I sighed. Unfortunately, she was right.

"I should have brought my gun," she breathed out.

"No, you shouldn't," I argued.

I also hated guns. Wouldn't touch them, avoided them at all costs, but Reese had carried one for as long as I knew him. My father and brother also carried. It was just part of them, so I was used to them to a certain degree.

Paisley rolled her eyes. "We're here to have fun. Let's have some fun…but let's do it inside. I'm freezing."

We all climbed out and donned jackets just as Reese walked our way and wrapped his arms around me. "You okay?"

I nodded, snuggling against his chest. "I am now."

"I've got you, baby."

I smiled. "I know."

"Good."

We headed inside, changed and then met by the fireplace about an hour later. Hawk and Payton joined us, looking like they'd stepped into their room for some fun of their own.

I smiled at her, knowing she'd obviously used her womanly wiles on her husband in order to distract him, which also meant she got something out of that tactic as well.

By the time we returned to our rooms to dress for dinner, the subject of the attack had changed to more pleasant conversation, however, Dallas insisted he and Macey walk us back to our room.

Reese went in first, making sure the room was clear, then he waited until I was inside before pulling the door closed. Reese locked it and we headed into the shower.

He guided me inside and wrapped an arm around my waist, sliding his other hand between my legs. I gasped when his thumb slid over my clit.

"Fuck, baby," he breathed as he slipped two fingers inside of me. "You're so wet."

I giggled. "I wonder how that happened."

Reese chuckled and stepped under the showerhead, running his hands through his hair before pulling me to him and turning me into the spray. He lathered his hands with shampoo and gently washed then conditioned my hair, then he poured body wash onto his hands and ran it over my back.

He wrapped his hands around me from behind and cupped my soapy breasts, working my nipples into hard peaks with his fingers. I arched into his touch.

"So good," I whispered as he slid his hand between my legs again.

"Turn around, baby."

I braced my hands on his shoulders and wrapped my legs around his waist as he lifted me, anchoring my back to the wall. I let out a deep breath as his girth filled me, his tip feeling as though it was touching my womb.

"Too much?"

I shook my head and leaned down to kiss him. His tongue met mine while his hands gripped my bottom, digging into the flesh. One arm slid up my back and cupped the base of my skull holding me steady while he began to move.

"Reese," I whimpered.

"Need me to slow down?"

"No. God, it's amazing."

The gentleness of his earlier movement changed and he began to thrust deeper, faster, harder, my arms locked around his neck as my body quickened. I felt my orgasm build and slid my hands into his hair, gripping his head as I screamed on my climax.

He thrust again and then pulsed inside of me, before pulling out gently and lowering my feet to the shower floor. "You okay?" he asked with a smile.

I leaned up on my tiptoes and kissed him. "So, so okay, honey."

"You scared?"

I shook my head. "I know you've got my back, sugar bear."

Reese tipped my chin up higher. "Always, right?"

"Always," I confirmed.

He kissed me gently and we dressed for dinner.

Paisley

SERGEI AND I ran into each other as we headed to dinner and we fell into our weird and edgy relationship. I knew he had a thing for me, which would never work, considering he was a total man-whore and I had no interest in being the one he wedded, bedded, then kept his mistress on the side like his dad had done. Men like Sergei didn't change.

Before we reached the dining room, however, Sergei shoved me into an alcove and I squeaked, slapping his arm. "What—"

His hand landed over my mouth and he leaned down. "Shhh. I'm trying to listen."

I scowled at him, but didn't speak and he removed his hand, keeping me against the wall and his body facing the hallway. Angry Russian voices carried and Sergei seemed interested in the subject at hand.

"What's going on?" I whispered.

"Pa, shush," he hissed.

"Start talking or I'm walking."

He faced me and narrowed his eyes. "Two men are arguing over my sister. Now, if you could just stay quiet for ten seconds so I can find out why, that'd be great."

"Oh." I swallowed. This was bad. This was very, very bad. "What are they saying?"

"Shut up," he mouthed angrily.

"Don't you dare speak to me that way," I hissed.

"I'll apologize later, but right now, I need you to let me listen."

He peeked his head slowly from our hiding place, and after about ten seconds, abruptly snapped it back in.

"Holy shit."

"What is it?" I asked.

"Two massive hotel porters, only I don't think they're on the hotel's payroll," he said, his face pale.

"What are they saying?"

"They're pissed. Something about not knowing how many people would be here with Alexa. They're talking about demanding more money for the job when they get back. I bet these are the guys that grabbed Payton. Oh my god, we have to get to my sister right away."

* * *

Reese

I was on high alert as we made our way to dinner. Hawk didn't like that some asshole had attacked his woman, and as much as Payton tried to brush it off, I was convinced someone had found out we were here and were gunning for Alexa.

New rule: no going anywhere without me.

Alexa hadn't even tried to argue, which indicated to me that she was more frightened than she was letting on. I didn't like that.

We approached the elevator and I saw a group of people waiting to ride, so I guided her toward the stairs instead.

"My legs are a little gelatinous, honey…why are we walking?"

"Too many people."

She stopped on the landing and faced me, laying her hand on my chest. "Honey, no one's going to attack us in the elevator."

"Not taking any chances."

She rolled her eyes. "Reese. You know my opinion on walking…and stairs are my undoing, so let's just catch the next elevator."

"I'm not opposed to carrying you, baby."

"You're going to carry me several flights down? Are you insane?"

I turned my back. "Hop up."

She placed her hands on my shoulders and wrapped her legs around my waist, and I started down the stairs. She wore jeans, so she wouldn't have to worry about flashing anyone during her piggyback ride.

"You're insane," she said with a giggle.

We made it to the lobby and I set her on her feet, dramatically leaning against the wall like I couldn't catch my breath.

"Oh, suck it Reese."

I laughed and pulled her away from prying eyes for a kiss. "Love you, baby."

"I love you, too, even though you're mean."

We made our way through the grand dining room, to our table, and joined the others already seated. The only ones missing were Paisley and Sergei.

"See, baby, we're not the last to arrive."

"Where *are* my brother and Paisley?"

"You don't think Sergei finally wore Paisley down, do you? Maybe she's admitted her true feelings for him and they're back in his room—"

"Ew, stop it," Alexa squeaked out in horror. "Believe me when I tell you that will *never* happen."

Just then, the devils of which we were speaking about arrived at the table. They were clearly flustered, looked entirely suspicious, and said absolutely nothing as they sat down. I was about to ask what they could have possibly been up to when Paisley shot me a look that said, *don't you dare say a word.*

"Everyone act naturally," Paisley finally said quietly.

"Why wouldn't we?" Dallas asked.

"Because there are two assassins here at the hotel, hired by the Russian mob, to kill Alexa."

I stiffened, but tried not to react further. "Who and where?" I asked coolly.

"I don't know where they are now. They're posing as hotel porters, but you can't miss them, they're real Hans and Franz types," Sergei said. "We overheard them arguing in Russian in the hallway when we were on our way to dinner. The little I could overhear was very clear to me. They're here to kill Lex and the rest of us are in the way."

"Okay, here's what we're going to do," Dallas said calmly. "We're going to order dinner and drinks, and have the time of our lives. I'll tell the waiter to water down the alcohol and be slow on the rounds. I want to be sharp, but don't want to tip these bastards off if they're watching us. We'll stick together and keep our eyes open. We're going to be the last group to leave this dining room and no one leaves this table until we leave together. Everyone got it?"

We all nodded and proceeded to act as casually as we possibly could under the circumstances. We ate a fantastic wild boar ragu, and drank shitty, watered down scotch, and conversed among ourselves until we were the last one's standing, or sitting as it were.

"Will that be all for the ladies and gentlemen?" Our unusually cheery waiter, Ned, asked. Most would have 86'd us around the time the vacuum cleaners fired up.

"Not quite, Ned," Dallas said softly and slowly. "I'm agent Dallas Stone with the FBI and I need you to listen to me very closely."

Dallas discreetly flashed his ID, and Ned's perma-grin instantly dropped.

"Nope, we're smiling. We're just gonna keep on smiling, Ned, because everything's totally normal to anyone who may be watching us," Dallas said softly.

Ned's eyes began to nervously dart around as he tried pathetically to re-form a smile.

"That's it. You're doing great, buddy. Now, I need you to make sure that any remaining dining and kitchen staff quietly exit through the kitchen's back door. If you see a staff member you don't know, don't approach them. If you understand, smile and nod."

Ned nodded slowly and then exited through the kitchen door.

Dallas's plan was to eliminate the number of potential bystanders that could be harmed should these thugs make a move. However, his plan had one weakness. With everyone out of the room, we were left very exposed.

"Okay, let's all casually stand up and then we're going to make our way through the kitchen, and out the back exit," Dallas said.

We did as instructed, and casually formed a barrier around Alexa as we walked in a tight group toward the kitchen. Dallas and I were first through the kitchen's double doors and immediately saw two huge men moving quickly toward us through the empty kitchen carrying baseball bats.

"Hans and Franz I presume," I said to Dallas.

"That's what I'm thinkin'," he agreed.

We pushed Alexa and the others back through the swinging doors, into the dining room. Dallas went for his gun, but before he could raise it, Hans delivered a blow to his right bicep. The gun fell to the floor, sliding under a large stainless-steel shelving unit.

"*Poluchit' yego!*" he yelled to his comrade, who was now closing in on me. He had a huge scar on his forehead and I immediately recognized him as the piece of shit I had beamed with the tear gas canister back at the Spiders' compound. With no time to dig for Dallas's gun, I grabbed the first thing within reach; a large cast iron skillet. I raised it over my head just as Franz tried to brain me with his Louisville Slugger. The bat connected with the skillet with a loud clang and sent shockwaves of pain from my hands to my shoulders.

"You motherfucker, I'm gonna make you pay for what you did to my face," he spit out.

"Looks like an improvement to me," I said, and hurled the heavy skillet at him. He sidestepped to avoid it, and was momentarily thrown off balance. I lunged at him, tackling him to the ground, and rained down punches to his face.

These guys were clearly trying to avoid the attention of gunfire, but I'm not sure the ensuing calamity inside the kitchen was much quieter. Hawk pushed through the double doors and headed straight for Hans, who was loading up for another swing at Dallas. He threw a huge overhand right and connected with the large Russian's jaw, causing him to stagger backward.

I heard Hawk yell, "Get down on the ground."

I turned to see Hawk had his gun drawn on Hans. I glanced up momentarily to see Dallas, now standing over me, his recovered gun pointing at the man I was currently pummeling.

"It's okay Reese, I got him," Dallas said, trying to get me to stop.

I grabbed the bloody thug by his coat and pulled him close to me. "Who the fuck sent you? Who hired you?" I yelled, to no avail. He was barely conscious at this point. I let him fall to the floor and Dallas cuffed him while Hawk zip-tied his prisoner.

We led our prisoners into the dining room and Dallas sat a still dazed Franz down on a chair. Alexa quickly began advancing at Hans, her eyes burning with rage, but before she could reach her would-be-assassin, he delivered a straight kick to her ribs, sending her to the floor.

"Lex!" I shouted and punched that piece of shit in the jaw as hard as I could. I heard his teeth hit the dining room floor just before he did.

"God damn it, Alexa," I hissed.

She groaned and curled up into the fetal position as I reached her.

"I'm okay," she whispered.

"Get her upstairs," Macey ordered. "I'll come and look at her in a bit."

I nodded and lifted Lex into my arms, carrying her

up to our room and trying not to lose my mind with every painful whimper she made.

* * *

Alexa

I hissed in pain when Reese lifted my shirt. "Let me see, baby."

"Ow, ow, *ow*!" I snapped when Reese prodded my bruised side. I wasn't sure whose way my ribs got in the way of, probably Hans, but whoever it was, their foot hurt like a mofo.

"I don't think anything's broken, but maybe Macey should have a look," he said.

"I'm okay, honey. I'll just put some ice on it."

He gave me a slight smile. "Badass to the core, huh?"

"Oh, is that the impression I gave you?"

"Little bit, baby."

"Well, right now I'm in too much pain to feel much like anything other than a damsel in distress." He scowled and I gingerly stretched out on the bed. "I'm okay, honey."

"I'm getting Macey now."

"Okay."

"Shit, seriously? Fuck. You really must be hurt if you're admitting you need to see a nurse," he deduced, opening the fridge to grab ice.

"I'll live…I think."

Reese wrapped ice in a towel and settled it on my side…I gasped at the cold, but then there was instant relief, so I was able to relax a little. He then called Macey before facing me on the bed and ran a finger gently down my cheek. "I'm so sorry."

"Why are *you* sorry?"

"Because I didn't stop you from running into the asshole's foot."

I sighed. "That wasn't my finest hour."

"Lex—"

A knock at the door interrupted whatever he was going to say, and he slid off the bed and opened the door. Macey walked in and immediately made her way over to me. "You're in pain?"

"A little," I lied.

"Okay, let's have a look."

She prodded my side gently and I tried not to react, but it hurt, damn it.

"Okay, honey, I think you might have a broken rib."

"I'm sure it's just bruised," I countered.

"We'd need an X-ray to confirm."

"Or we can bind me up tight and go from there."

"*Lex,*" Reese ground out.

"I'm fine, honey. Just leave it."

"You really need to get some Vicodin or Percocet, Lex. If you don't, you won't be able to take deep breaths and that could lead to a bronchial infection."

"Do you have any?" I asked, hopefully.

"No. You should see a doctor."

"I'll be good."

"You're going to see a doctor," Reese said, and picked up the phone.

"You'll have to explain what happened, honey."

"Let me call Alec and see if he'll call something in. Dallas and I can pick it up for you."

"Thanks, Macey," I rasped. "Before you do that, though, can you please check Reese's hand?"

"I'm good."

"Don't think I didn't notice how bloody and bruised up it is," I argued.

"I'm fine, baby."

Macey held her hand out, palm up. "Show me."

He sighed and did as she ordered, and I could tell he was biting back pain as Macey gave him the once-over. "I don't think anything's broken, but again, I'm not a human X-ray, and I think you should have it looked at."

"I'll wrap it and we can take care of it when we get back if it's still buggin' me."

"You're as bad as Dallas," she complained.

Reese smiled. "I'll take that as a compliment."

"Don't." She rolled her eyes and focused on me with a smile. "I'll let you know what Alec says. If he refuses to call in something, I'll sic Dallas on him."

"That's what brothers are for," Reese said with a smile. "Thanks, Macey."

"No problem. Keep icing, Lex."

"I will," I promised. "Thanks for everything."

Macey nodded and left our room. Reese stretched out beside me, kissing me gently. "Think you can sleep?"

"I'm going to try."

He nodded and helped me undress, then he took me back to bed and I fell into a fitful and pain-filled sleep.

Alexa

WE WERE HOME. Our home. We'd been off the mountain for about a month and all was returning to normal…sort of. Reese's friend, Frogger was almost completely recovered from his gunshot wounds and he'd just left our home after sharing dinner with us. I was now snuggled up to Reese on the sofa watching one of the Star Wars movies. I couldn't tell you which one because I couldn't seem to stay awake.

"Let's go to bed," Reese said.

"No, I'm good. I'm awake."

He chuckled. "I can tell."

"We can finish the movie."

"Are you in pain?"

"Nope."

"Are you lyin'?"

"A little." I smiled up at him. "But I'm okay. I want to be completely done with those meds."

"You can take one before we go to bed, but you're not waitin' all night."

"Yes, sir." I gave him a salute, regretting the movement the second I did it.

"Baby," he admonished. "You're takin' one now."

He rose to his feet and grabbed my pills from the kitchen. He handed me one with a glass of water and I took it, then he insisted we head to bed.

My rib injury was actually pissing me off. We'd been forced to have "careful" relations for the past several weeks and I was over it, quite frankly. As soon as I felt good enough for activity, I pushed myself and felt like I undid all the progress.

"Do we really need to go to bed?"

"What else would you like to do?" he asked.

"Fuck."

He dropped his head back and groaned. "Alexa."

"Yes, honey?"

"We can't."

"You'll be careful."

"Baby, there's no way in hell."

I bit my lip. "What about a little oral?"

"Lex."

"I bet your protein would help me heal," I said. "Like in all the superhero movies…your cum is the key."

"Fuck me."

"Yes, please."

He groaned. "Stop, Lex."

"I haven't done anything."

He frowned. "Your dirty mouth is the problem

here, baby, and you know it."

"It's fine, Reese." I raised my hands in surrender. "Just put it on record that you're the one denying me my wifely right."

Before I got the chance to rant again, his mouth was on mine and my panties and shorts were shoved off my body.

"On the bed, Lex. Carefully. If you hurt, you tell me."

I nodded, but to be honest, if Reese was between my legs in any capacity, I wouldn't want him to stop, even if I was in pain. I climbed onto the bed and settled my back against the pillows. Reese knelt between my legs and pushed my knees open, covering my core with his mouth.

I mewed and arched into his mouth as he continued his delicious assault, sucking my clit then blowing gently. His thumb replaced his mouth for a brief second, then his fingers slipped inside of me and I had his tongue again. I whimpered as my orgasm built, wanting him to never stop.

"Come, baby," he ordered, and I did.

He slid off the bed and removed his clothes, his cock springing free, and I licked my lips.

"I'm gonna let you take the lead, yeah?"

"Oh, *yeah*," I breathed out.

He chuckled, stretching out on his back and I shifted so I was straddling him. He guided his cock into me and I anchored my hands on his chest and lowered myself so I could draw him deeper inside of me.

"Baby," he whispered, sliding one hand between us to finger me.

I raised up and then lowered myself again, smiling

down at him. "I love you."

"Kiss me," he demanded, so I leaned down to kiss him gently. "You okay?"

"I'm good, honey." I rocked against him, staying chest to chest which shifted the angle of his cock. "So, so good."

I pressed into his fingers and rocked gently, pushing up for more leverage. With my hands on his chest, I dropped my head back as he brought me to the edge and then over the cliff. I cried out his name as I came around him, and settled against his body again. He thrust a couple more times and then his cock pulsed inside of me and he wrapped his arms around my waist gently.

"Perfect," I whispered.

"You feel better now?" he retorted.

"Sort of."

"What?"

I met his eyes. "Well, it was great, don't get me wrong…it just wasn't…"

"Wasn't what?"

"Dirty."

He laughed, shaking my body as he did. "Damn, Lex, I thought you were sayin' I didn't satisfy you."

"You *always* satisfy me. I just like it better when you fuck me from behind and beat the shit out of my ass."

He hissed, squeezing his eyes shut and I grinned as he hardened inside of me again. My little plan had worked, so now maybe I'd get the spanking I was really craving.

He opened his eyes again and studied me. "You really want this?"

I bobbed my head up and down.

"Okay, baby, on your knees. But if you hurt, we stop."

"No," I said, climbing off of him.

"I'm not doin' this unless you promise."

"*Reese*."

"Promise me, Lex."

I groaned in irritation, shifting so I was on all fours. "*Fine*, I promise."

Reese positioned himself behind me and slid slowly into me. I mewed, pressing back against him.

"You okay?"

"I'm great," I said. "More, honey. *Please* don't be gentle."

He slammed into me, his palm slapping me and the sensation overtook everything. God, it felt amazing, but when he slid one hand between my legs and fingered my clit, I came the second the palm of his other hand slapped against my ass again, and I cried out his name as I buried my face in the mattress while he continued to thrust into me. His body locked and he wrapped his arms around me, gently rolling us to the side so we were spooning, staying connected as he kissed the back of my neck.

"Are you hurtin'?"

"Not even a little bit." I sighed. "That was exactly what I needed."

"Well, I aim to please."

I giggled. "Ow."

"Alexa," he growled.

"I'm okay. I just forgot to brace." I broke our connection and gingerly rolled to face him. "I'm good, sugar bear. Especially now."

He smiled, stroking my cheek. "Hate that you're in pain."

"I know, honey, but I feel a little better every day. And every orgasm helps."

Reese chuckled. "You should make a PSA."

"That might be a good idea."

"Are you nervous about Monday?"

Monday was the day set for me to testify. Reese had me "locked up" close to him, which I didn't mind so much since I loved our home, but I couldn't wait for all of this to be over so I could come and go freely.

"I'm not nervous so much as I'm scared shitless," I admitted.

He sighed. "Yeah, me too, baby."

"You're not supposed to say that," I complained.

"Regardless of how I'm feeling, I've got you."

I burrowed closer to him. "I know."

"We're gonna spend the weekend doing nothing, okay?" he said. "Just you and me and some movies."

"And ice cream."

"Yeah, Freckles, and ice cream."

"I like that, husband."

He chuckled. "That's good, wife."

"For now, I'd really appreciate it if you fed me."

"I can do that."

We commenced naked food time and I forced myself to forget about the trial for the moment.

* * *

Monday morning, we walked into the courthouse with an army behind us. Well, it probably looked like an army, since it was pretty much all of Reese's crew, plus a dozen Dogs who came to support me.

Reese held my hand and we sat in the hallway while the mob headed into the courtroom. I had to wait until called to testify and wasn't allowed into the proceedings until it was my turn. Hawk waited with us for "extra protection."

We'd been in the hallway about ten minutes when Dallas Stone walked toward us, a tall dark-headed man next to him.

"That's Brock," Reese said. "Dallas's partner and Payton's brother."

"He looks like Payton."

"Of course you'd notice that." Reese stood and held his hand out with a chuckle.

I took his hand and rose to my feet just as the men walked up to us.

"Why are you out here?" Dallas asked, sounding a little miffed.

"What do you mean?" I asked.

"You should be sequestered…somewhere safe," he said.

Before he could say more, a flustered man in a suit came rushing up to us. "Ms. Romanov."

"Mrs. Alden," I corrected.

"Oh, ah, sorry…and congratulations."

I nodded.

"I'm Meryl Winthrop, and I'm assisting the D.A. with this case. We have a private room set up for you to wait."

"We'll be accompanying her," Dallas said.

"I don't know—"

"It's not up for discussion," Brock said.

"Hmm, he sounds like you," I mused to Reese. He rolled his eyes but said nothing.

"If you'll follow me," Meryl said, and led us away from the courtroom doors.

We walked down a hallway and then through a series of doors, ending up in a small, quiet room with just one window.

"Is this room secure?" Dallas asked.

"Ah…yes, sir. Very," Meryl said.

"We'll be right outside, Lex," Dallas said.

I nodded and sat in one of the chairs by the wall.

"The door back there leads to a private restroom. There's also coffee and some pastries, please help yourself," Meryl offered. "I'll come and collect you when it's time."

"Okay, thank you, Mr. Winthrop," I said.

He nodded and left me alone with Reese.

Reese waited two-point-three seconds before he poured himself a cup of coffee and grabbed a bear claw. I chuckled. "Sure, honey, I'd love some coffee and a bear claw."

"There's only one bear claw."

"I noticed."

"I licked it," he said.

"I noticed that, too."

Reese chuckled. "Well, if you still want it, you can have it."

I sighed. "No, it's okay, I'm good."

He set his treat down and hunkered down in front of me. "It's all gonna be over in a matter of hours."

"Unless I have to testify tomorrow."

"Well, let's hope for the best." He rose to his feet again. "The coffee's not bad for a government establishment, so how about I make you a cup and we can split the bear claw?"

I nodded, although, I wasn't sure I'd be able to eat.

We were stuck in our little prison for the next two hours and then it was time. Meryl led me down the hallway and I felt like a lamb being led to slaughter.

* * *

Three hours later, I was excused, and the judge called recess until the morning.

"You ready to go get dinner?" Reese asked.

I shook my head. "I want you to take me home."

"Okay, baby. We can do that."

"And to bed…but not to sleep."

"We can definitely do that," he said.

Due to traffic, we arrived home a little later than expected, but it didn't matter, it was done…at least for the day. Reese closed and locked the front door, then his mouth was on mine and I was in his arms, my legs wrapped around his waist. He carried me to our room where he tore my clothes off, and his mouth settled between my legs, sucking my clit, his tongue swirling as he added pressure with each pass he made.

He slid his fingers inside of me and my body shivered. Then I lost his mouth and I whimpered. Reese finished removing his clothes before he climbed up my body, linking his fingers with mine and holding them over my head, and then pushed into me. I sighed as I wrapped my legs around him and arched up. He slammed into me over and over again and it was sweeter than it had been, more emotional than it ever had been, and I didn't think I could love him more.

"Reese…" I came undone and he kissed me, releasing one of my hands to stroke my neck as we climaxed, and anchored me to him as he rolled us to the side.

His hand cupped my bottom and he kissed my temple. "Love you."

"Ohmigod, I love you more."

He chuckled. "I highly doubt that."

I rolled and shifted so I was straddling him.

He slid his hand between us and thumbed my clit. I dropped my head back and rocked against him. "Grab the headboard, Lex."

I did as I was told and he slid down so his face was between my legs, lifting his head up so his mouth covered my core. I pressed my body down, but he gripped my hips and anchored me where he wanted me.

"So fuckin' wet, baby," he rasped, and sucked my clit.

"Yeah, I *know*," I retorted.

He repositioned me so I was on all fours. "Cheek to the mattress, Lex."

I obeyed immediately and he lifted my bottom, sliding his finger over my wetness and moved it to my very forbidden area.

"Finger your clit, baby," he ordered, and I reached back.

His cock slid inside me, slowly at first, and I worked my clit while he tortured my pussy. "Reese!"

"Brace, baby."

I grabbed the edge of the mattress and he slammed into me, harder and harder. "I'm—"

"Don't come," he ordered.

"Reese!" I hissed.

He slapped my bottom, which *really* didn't help. "Don't come, Lex."

I tried to keep my orgasm at bay, but then his finger slid into the tightness of my ass and I exploded, screaming his name into the pillow as I collapsed onto the mattress. Reese rolled us to our sides again, staying connected as he continued to move, his hand sliding between my legs and cupping my mound as he worked my clit. I didn't have enough breath to speak.

While one hand worked my clit, his other rolled my nipple into a tight bud and he slammed into me, building yet another orgasm.

"Come, baby," he whispered, and I let go.

I felt him pulse inside of me and then he kissed my shoulder and held me tight.

"This all just gets so much better," I whispered.

"Yeah, baby, it does." He slid out of me and made his way to the bathroom, bringing a warm washcloth back to clean me up.

"Thanks for having my back, honey," I said.

"Always."

"I know, but I needed to thank you anyway."

He smiled, climbing up beside me and pulling me into his arms. "You did great, baby. Concise, to the point, and you didn't let the defense attorney rattle you."

"Well, he's a dick…and I imagined him in a leather mask with a ball gag in his mouth. It helped."

Reese laughed. "Seriously?"

"Seriously." I smiled. "The underwear thing didn't work. I kept seeing his big ol' stomach hanging over a pair of tighty whities and it grossed me out."

"Yeah. I see what you mean."

I kissed his chest. "I could always try a ball gag on you."

Reese groaned, rolling me on my back. "Hard no for me."

I giggled. "Are you *sure*?"

"Hundred percent, Alexa."

I sighed dramatically. "Bummer."

He grinned, sliding his hand to my bottom.

"Am I in trouble?" I asked hopefully.

"Do you want to be?"

"Ohmigod, yes."

He gave me one very satisfying smack before making love to me again, dirty, just the way I liked it. I knew his goal was to distract me and he did it perfectly, keeping my mind off the trial for several hours.

Unfortunately, I was called back the next day for a few follow-up questions and that made me more nervous than the initial testimony.

Alexa

THE NEXT AFTERNOON, we arrived at the courthouse thirty minutes before I was due to testify. At least I'd had the morning to relax…my interview time had been pushed back until two. We were ushered to our little prison again, only this time, Summer was sequestered with us.

"Oh, my goodness, I'm so glad you're here," she said, and hugged me.

I studied her. Her face was a little red and her eyes looked puffy, like she'd been crying. "Are you okay?"

She nodded. "Yes. I just had a really rough morning."

"Oh no…did 'ball gag' get the best of you?"

Reese choked back a laugh.

Summer frowned. "Huh?"

"The defense attorney."

"Oh, yes. He was really mean, but I handled him. No, I got a call from my sister. She's in the hospital."

"What happened?"

She bit her lip. "Car accident. But I can't leave until I'm excused."

"That doesn't sound fair."

"I know," she said.

"Let me see what I can find out," Reese offered and left the room.

"Who brought you here?" I asked.

"Um, someone named Dallas. Super cute."

"Yeah, he is." I smiled. "Also super married."

She sighed. "They always are."

I giggled. "Not always."

"Well, considering you married one, I beg to differ."

I heard a popping sound outside the door, then Reese rushed in, followed by Dallas.

"Get in the bathroom," Reese demanded. "Lock the door and stay there until I come and get you."

"What's going on?" I asked, jumping to my feet.

Reese pushed me and Summer through the door. "Just stay here."

"Ohmigod, Reese, you need to tell me what the hell is going on!"

"Shooters," he snapped. "*Stay* here."

He pulled the door closed and I faced Summer who now looked like she wanted to kill someone…not the reaction I expected.

"You okay?" I asked.

"I swear to *god*," she ground out. "If I have to come back and do this all over again, I will annihilate those damn Russians! They're behind this and I am so over it."

Okay, so Summer's a badass. Good to know.

She reached for the door, but I stepped in front of it. "You can't go out there."

"Why not?" she snapped.

"*Um*, because you could get shot," I returned. "I kind of like you, Summer, so please don't be an idiot."

"I want them to pay, Alexa," she seethed. "I'm so sick of them hijacking my life!"

"I know," I admitted with a sigh. "I totally get it."

"But you get to go home to your gorgeous man every day. I have to go back to the abbey because my life is no longer my life." She paced the small bathroom. "I was happy. I had a great job…yes, I know it wasn't real, but I didn't know that back then…I had a gorgeous apartment overlooking the Willamette, and I had friends. A *lot* of friends! I'd just met a great guy and we were ready to take it to the next level, but *no*. Those fucking Russians ruined my life, Lex. *Ruined* it!"

"Okay, I hear you. But can I just point something out?"

"No."

"Okey doke," I said.

She huffed. "What?"

"You said you didn't want me to point it out."

She waved her hand. "Just say it already."

"Well, you're twenty-six."

"Four."

"Twenty-four…you have a few more days of testimony and then I'm pretty sure you'll be able to leave the abbey."

"Unless they don't get convicted," she cried.

She had me there. I sighed. "I'm pretty sure they'll

get convicted."

"You don't know their reach."

"Oh, I think I do," I countered.

Summer sighed. "Right. Sorry."

"It's okay. I get it. Really. It'll all be over soon." I said all this, all the while knowing I'd had the same conversation with Reese not even a week ago. I was over being on house arrest and wanted to go out to dinner or to a movie, but I had to stay sequestered in our home. A home I loved, yes, but I didn't like being forced to stay there. A gilded cage, despite how beautiful, was still a cage.

The door slammed open and I couldn't stop a scream, but it was Reese, who pulled me in for a hug and kissed my temple. "It's okay, baby."

"What happened?"

"Hans and Franz two-point-oh decided to give the courthouse a visit."

The original Hans and Franz were sitting in a federal holding cell awaiting trial. We hadn't seen them since our honeymoon.

"Is anyone hurt?" I asked, checking Reese for injuries.

"I'm fine, Lex. One of the cops got shot, but he had a vest on, so he just got winded. They took the guys down and are assessing any other potential injuries. That's all I know right now."

"Are we still going to testify today?" Summer asked.

"Don't know," Reese said. "We're waitin' until they clear the building."

"Assholes," she hissed.

"Indeed."

I held Reese tighter, the fear suddenly setting in,

and my body started shaking.

"Okay, baby, I've got you," he whispered.

"Is this *ever* going to stop?"

"Yeah, baby. It's stoppin' now."

"They're going to keep coming."

He stroked my hair. "Not if we cut the head off the snake."

"Except for every head you cut off, a new one grows."

He sighed. "I don't give a shit about new ones. I just want the one whose radar you're on."

I wrapped my arms around his waist and leaned heavily against him.

"Reese!" Dallas called.

"In here, man." He released his hold on me, but didn't go far. "All clear?"

"Yeah," Dallas said walking toward us. "But they're canceling session for the day...probably tomorrow too."

"Fuckers," Summer hissed. "Are you going to kill these people, Dallas?"

He smiled. "Wish I could, Summer."

"Pussy."

"Whoa," I said. "I think that's kind of harsh."

"Sorry, Dallas," she grumbled.

Dallas laughed. "I didn't take it personally. I get it."

"So, if I "found" someone to take care of the problem—"

My mouth dropped open of its own accord just as Dallas raised a hand. "Don't say shit like that to me, Summer. I'll have to lock you up."

Summer mumbled a few expletives and Dallas and Reese ushered us out of the room and to a back exit currently under heavy guard. After the men showed their credentials, we were allowed to leave and I was whisked home, while Summer was taken back to the abbey.

* * *

Two weeks later, it was over. Summer and I had our final day of testimony six days ago. The jury had deliberated for two days and then come back with "guilty on all counts."

The men would never see freedom in their lifetime, and apparently one of them (I don't know which one) flipped on a couple of lower-level guys, so he had ten years shaved off his one-hundred-ninety-year sentence. The FBI mole had been locked up, and apparently, his spy brethren had made sure the prison population knew he'd been law-enforcement before his incarceration. His life was not going well, which suited me fine. Little bastard got a hell of a lot less than he deserved, in my opinion.

Paisley, Summer, and the rest of the ladies who testified would need to stay at the abbey for a few more weeks or so, but it meant Dallas and the rest of the FBI could smoothly transition them back to their lives. At least, that was the plan.

Summer's sister was home and healing from her car accident, and Dallas made sure Summer could see her on a regular basis, so Summer seemed calmer now that everyone was safe.

I'd been awakened by the call of my stomach rebelling and I currently had my head in the toilet for the third time in an hour.

"What can I do?" Reese asked from the open doorway.

"You can get me some saltines."

"Okay, baby, I'm gonna make a quick run to the store."

I nodded. "'K."

I didn't move until he got back and he was smart enough to buy a couple more pregnancy tests. I was late again, but figured it was the stress of the trial, so I expected another negative result…however, I was wrong.

Reese's face looked like it would explode with happy glitter. "You're pregnant."

"That's what it says."

"Take the other one just to make sure."

I giggled. "I'm kind of peed out, honey. Later."

"Love you, Freckles," he whispered, kissing me gently.

"Love you, too."

"I'm gonna feed you, then you're goin' back to bed to rest."

"I don't need to rest, honey."

"Humor me."

"You're not going to give me problems when I go back to work, are you?" I challenged. Cameron had filled my boss, Arthur, in on the kidnapping and some minor details after I was taken to the abbey, letting him know I'd be in protective custody for an indefinite period. Arthur had been incredibly gracious and offered me my job back the second I called to check-in with him.

"You're not going back to work."

"Reese," I admonished.

"You're pregnant."

I laughed. "Pregnant women work all the time."

"Not my pregnant woman."

“Ohmigod, sugar bear, I’m going nuts. I love working. I love everything about it. I *need* it,” I argued. “They held my job, Reese. I want to keep my end of the bargain.”

He sighed. “We’ll see what the doctor says about it.”

I rolled my eyes. “Okay, honey.” I knew the doctor would be fine with it, so I let Reese have his moment.

As Reese fed me a gourmet breakfast of saltines and Sprite, I made him join me in bed, which meant once I felt better, I was gonna get me some.

He protested for all of ten seconds and as he made love to me, I relished the feeling of being wholly loved and completely free.

Alexa

Three years later…

"WAIT UP, LITTLE man," Reese called as our two-year-old came barreling toward my very round belly.

Hudson Reese Alden had turned two close to six months ago, right around the time I found out I was pregnant with his little sister. Reese had just taken him to the park to run off some energy.

"Mama!" he squealed and I knelt to catch him.

"Hey, Bubba, how's my boy?"

"Wet," Reese replied. "We got caught in the downpour."

I chuckled, lifting Hudson, and carrying him to his room.

"Baby, let me do that," Reese said, pulling him away from me. "You shouldn't be lifting him."

"I'm good, honey."

"Sit down, Lex. I'll take care of it."

I rolled my eyes, but took a seat in the rocker by the bed. Hudson was an absolute mini-Reese, right down to the confident swagger anytime he walked into a room. I wondered who our daughter would take after and I kind of hoped she'd look like me. Hudson did have my eyes, but that's where the similarities ended.

I'd gone back to work, then took three months off with Hudson, and planned to take the same with the new baby, but Reese was pushing for me to quit and go into business for myself. I got it. He worked a lot of nights managing the bars, and I worked days, so we didn't have as much time to spend together and if I were working for myself, I'd have a more flexible schedule. At least, that was the theory.

"What time are Ryder and Sadie gonna be here?" Reese asked.

"Six."

Ryder and Sadie now had two kids of their own…two boys, who loved to spend time with their "cousin" Hudson.

"Okay, nap time for you, buddy," he said, and settled him in his crib. "Alone time for me and Mommy."

I shivered. I knew what that meant.

He pulled me up from the chair and we left the room and headed for ours. "Where do you want me to start, Lex."

I licked my lips. "On your back."

He grinned and stripped, stretching out on the bed so I could straddle him, the perfect position for me at the current time.

We made love and then I was ordered to nap before dinner. As I lost my fight with sleep, I couldn't help but smile.

It had been a long, rough wait for my perfect man, but it was worth it.

Piper Davenport writes from a place of passion and intrigue. Combining elements of romance and suspense with strong modern-day heroes and heroines. The Sinners and Saints novels are a spinoff of her celebrated Dogs of Fire Motorcycle Club Series.

She lives in the beautiful Pacific Northwest with her husband and two boys.

I hope you've enjoyed **Reese**
For information about my other titles, please visit:
www.facebook.com/piperdavenport

Find me on Twitter, too!
https://twitter.com/piper_davenport

Made in the USA
Columbia, SC
17 January 2023